Three

Easy-to-read stories with a powerful touch of the profound

By J S Morey

Love's Too Short
You Only Love Once
The Black Hound of Dartmoor

First published in Great Britain 2023

ISBN: 9798397867757

Three Easy Pieces

by J S Morey

Page 4: Love's Too Short

When your strongest of emotions have at last been realised, only for life's uncertain challenges waiting to intervene, you treasure the moments you do have.

Page 68: You Only Love Once

Impulse is the strangest thing - often devoid of reason yet, sometimes, by some amazing twist of fate or fortune it comes up with the right solution.

Sometimes...

Page 96: The Black Hound of Dartmoor

Set in south Dartmoor, this bewitching tale has its roots in truth and legend, leaving you to decide which is which.

Take a solitary walk on a dark night across any un-familiar - or even familiar - moorland landscape, and the truth element of this short story will find *you*.

Love's Too Short

A romantic mystery set against the backdrop of St Ives

J S Morey

First published in Great Britain 2023

Further reading:

The series 'Love should never be this hard':

Book 1: The Sign of the Rose
Book 2: The Black Rose of Blaby
Book 3: Rose: The Missing Years
Book 4: Finding Rose

Wild Hearts Roam Free – and Wild Hearts Come Home
Two modern westerns set in Wyoming

Unresolved? - a short story linked to 'Wild Hearts Roam Free'

Those Italian Girls – set in the hills of Tuscany

Read My Shorts – short stories and poems with a message

Wood-Spirit - an anthology of poems about trees

For more by this author
visit www.newnovel.co.uk

Chapter One

It was the end of his shift and the worst time for the wheels to come off his trolley. Actually it was just the one wheel.

But two breakfasts.

Either way it was enough for the plates to slide, topple, then crash to the floor in the hotel upstairs lobby just as he was emerging from the lift. The front wheel had caught on the lip of the fifth floor carpet, just enough to buckle the fragile caster even more.

Which was why the wheel had come off.

'Curses!' Jake cried as disaster struck. If losing the entire contents of two elaborate breakfasts wasn't enough, the delay serving the guests - *and* potentially jeopardising a handsome tip - only worsened the situation.

It was six thirty on an otherwise bright sunny morning at the height of the holiday season and Jake, the night porter, had an hour and a half to go before Ray, the *day* porter, took over. He'd already spent forty minutes in the Still Room preparing each ingredient to perfection. Even though he had some left over or partially cooked, he'd promised himself the same treat, including the kedgeree, before ending his shift. That luxury had disappeared too but he left the mess where it lay, seeping into the carpet.

He'd clear it up later.

He remembered the golden mantra learnt on Day

One of his hotel management training: guests' comfort and satisfaction must come first. Muttering those words almost silently to himself he took the lift back to the ground floor kitchen, mentally going through the step-by-step process he had to begin all over again in for the 'Luxury Breakfast - (2) - *Edition Two*.

Before re-entering the kitchen he grabbed another trolley. The breakfast room would still be empty of guests for another half hour at least. Even waiters had yet to appear - thankfully, to save his blushes - since they'd laid each table the evening before at the end of their own shift.

But he didn't escape the eagle eye of the assistant manager. He was always early, if only to check Jake completed all the tasks he'd lined up for him during the quiet hours of the previous night, and to be completed after the rest of the staff had left. That was usually just after midnight unless Jake kept the barman late for a 'lock-in'.

'What on earth was that noise?' hissed the assistant manager, Geoff Larkin, through clenched teeth. 'It's a miracle you didn't wake up the whole hotel!' He'd quickly and silently slid out from the laundry room, sneaking up behind Jake on purpose to make him jump.

'Jeez-us,' cried Jake. 'I wish you wouldn't do that.'

Larkin winced and glared at Jake but said nothing - his look was just enough to register he considered

Jake's outburst insubordinate. Insolent. After two months working together it was clear there was a mutual disrespect between the two. Larkin was the more senior and, technically, his boss; but Jake was taller, more solidly built, and not used to being messed with under different circumstances, regardless of rank.

Larkin couldn't let him off the hook entirely.

'Remember this is a five star establishment,' he stressed, 'and Lord Rees is one of our best customers. I take it you delivered his breakfast safely.'

'Almost,' Jake lied. 'I forgot the coffee and toast.'

He was expecting a full interrogation from Larkin as to why he'd made so much clatter a few moments earlier - loud enough to carry over four floors - until suddenly distracted by the opening of the same door to the laundry room. For a second time.

It was one of the chamber-maids.

Seeing Jake, she hurriedly continued fastening the last two buttons of her blouse before scurrying upstairs carrying towels and pillow cases. Larkin was clearly flustered.

'We'll say no more about this and your lack of...,' he began, then, 'well anyway, get the rest of Lord Rees' breakfast.'

'*The sleaze*,' thought Jake as he headed for the Still Room for the second time that morning. Then he brightened up just a little bit as he realised, '*Now I've got some leverage over you, Geoffy-Boy!*'

But he couldn't stop feeling sorry for the chamber-maid whom he considered 'could do better'. In fact, *'any girl could do better than Larkin,'* he concluded.

He was relieved to see Chef had turned up early, greeting Jake cheerfully as he entered the kitchen.

'Come back for seconds?'

'How did you guess?' replied Jake.

Chef was one of the few staff who had a room in the hotel - in one of the attic rooms, *above* the fifth floor. He'd not only heard the crash - he was up and shaving at the time - but he had to step past what was left of the breakfasts, and the broken trolley, on his way down the back stairs

'I'll help you get another trolley-load ready.' Chef scanned the breakfast order ticket and set about preparing replacements, sharing the task with Jake.

Fifteen minutes later Jake was almost good to go - for the second time. He was running a little late but Chef helped him out with that, too. While the second lot of kedgeree was cooking he called Lord Rees' room.

A still-yawning Lady Rees answered.

'Lady Rees?'

'Who's this?' She yawned a second time.

'Sorry if I've woken you,' Chef apologised, 'but your room service is ready. May we bring it up now?'

'Dennis? Are you still in the shower?' She was calling out to her husband so, luckily, they clearly were *not* quite ready. She'd had her hand over the receiver but now came back to Chef. 'It's a *bit* early. Could you give us ten minutes?'

Chef agreed, replaced the receiver, giving Jake the thumbs up as he did so. Perfect. They wouldn't be seen to be late after all. After a few minutes Jake was headed for the lift with a *sound* trolley loaded with two replacement Luxury Breakfasts.

Chef was one of 'the good guys'. He and Jake had struck up a friendship almost immediately. Jake needed to understand all roles in the hotel as part of his training - which included knowledge of how an efficient kitchen was run. Chef regarded it as a bonus rather than an intrusion that someone was interested in 'his world' and would even help out by teaching Jake some of the tricks of his trade.

It was to pay off for Chef that very morning, soon rewarded for his kindness.

The Second Chef happened to ring in while Jake was upstairs with Lord and Lady Rees to ask if he could come in late. He had to take his children to school that particular day, leaving Chef with all the breakfasts to prepare and relying on just one kitchen porter. But that's where Jake's availability - and enthusiasm for the job - came in today. He agreed to stay on until nine o'clock to cover for the Second Chef. Perfect.

It would also turn out well for Jake as he - finally - finished his shift just after nine o'clock, with another surprise in store.

'Hold on a moment, Jake.'

He was almost out the door at nine when Larkin's voice called him back. His first instinct was 'what now? until he noticed... he had someone with him.

A girl.

'Just the man I've been looking for,' Larkin went on to explain. 'I've got an emergency run to the wholesalers in Camborne. The Second Chef hasn't shown up. I need you to come with me. I've put my back out and there could be some heavy lifting - especially the tinned stuff. I can't do it alone and I can't expect Toni - here - to do it.'

He stepped to one side to bring 'the someone' to the fore. '*This* is Toni,' he said. 'She starts today on front of house, but she's to do some ordering from suppliers as part of her job.

'She's coming too.'

'Jake,' he announced, shaking her hand. He couldn't help but feel how long and slender her fingers were. But that wasn't her only feature he noticed. She had the softest blue eyes, but their mistiness belied a feeling that she could reach right into you. He flushed in embarrassment once he realised he was staring into them. His initial reaction would normally be to ask Larkin why Ray couldn't go to the wholesaler with him, even though he knew the day porter was needed for early check-outs and arrivals. Now, seeing this vision before him, he was glad he had - just for once - kept his mouth shut.

More than her eyes captivated him. Much more. *She* was gorgeous.

'Nice to meet you.' She, too, allowed her eyes to linger on his - 'for just a little longer than normal' he thought. It gave him an excuse to retain the hand-shake but he came to his senses, letting go of her hand certain that she - and maybe Larkin - could read his thoughts.

She eventually looked away.

'The van's out front,' broke in Larkin, conscious he was disturbing 'something' that had happened between Jake and Toni.

But what? His focus was usually much more basic.

He led the way to where the van was parked, dir-ectly outside the hotel. The warmth of the sun and the fact it was now approaching mid-morning hit Jake for the first time that day. He was also taken by how fair - blonde - Toni's hair was, as well as her skin - almost too pale. Clearly she hadn't had any chance to lay on the beach, as he'd been able to between shifts, even though it was early season.

Jake held open the passenger door for Toni, giving him another chance to touch her, to hold her forearm and support her as she negotiated the two steps into the cab, onto the three-seater bench.

Next to Larkin.

She was squashed *between* Jake and Larkin.

The motor fired up and the van lurched sideways.

Larkin swung round in the road, failing to execute a three point turn by hitting both curbs before heading towards Camborne. With no seat-belts or handle to hold the movement caused Toni to lean and press into Larkin - perhaps a deliberate move on Larkin's part, or so Jake suspected. He edged himself well over to the passenger side to give her more room. Was it out of chivalry, respect for Toni? good manners? or out of shyness? He'd certainly not felt like this for a girl - any girl - for a long time.

It was a good feeling.

Toni responded differently. She pressed herself *towards* Jake once the van was steady and cruising in a straight line. Now that *was* deliberate. He read the signals correctly. She was sending him a message.

It read, 'Save me from this creep'.

Or so he wished to believe.

The remainder of the journey was without incident. Jake pondered on the irony that Larkin had invited him along, given the predatory sleaze that he (Larkin) was when it came to attractive young girls - especially those over whom he had some 'control' due to his seniority and their dependence upon him for a job. Surely he wanted Toni all to himself, a chance to take advantage in the same way, or so it was rumoured he'd done in the past, or present, such as with the chamber-maid in the laundry room that very morning.

In the end, Jake concluded that Larkin's laziness

had over-ridden his sleaziness. Either that, or maybe Larkin's back really *was* troubling him - and he really did need Jake.

By the time they reached Camborne, Jake could feel the heat from Toni's thigh - she had now managed clear space between herself and Larkin. But they reached their destination all too soon for Jake. They parked and, as they got down from the van, he again caught hold of her arm.

Her smile was enough 'thanks' for him.

Once inside the wholesalers, Larkin again led the way, consulting his list and explaining each purchase to Toni whilst Jake followed obediently behind, aisle by aisle, pushing the trolley. Before long it was full as they headed for the check-out, the trolley groaning under the weight of food.

Hopefully, wheels would *not* fall off this time.

They didn't and, with the van suitably loaded - by Jake - they set off back to St Ives with Toni keeping comfortably close to him, away from Larkin.

It was noon when they reached the hotel and twelve thirty by the time Jake had carried in the last of the provisions. As much as he disliked being anywhere near Larkin, the opportunity to get to know 'the new girl' more than made up for it. Larkin witnessed the new attachment and, surprisingly, didn't resent it too much - despite Jake not being one of his favourite people. That said, it was hard to find anyone that Larkin *did* take to - unless they happened to be female

And below thirty years old.

'When does your shift end, Toni?' He liked the sound of her name, even to the point where he liked saying it. They were alone in the hotel lobby. Larkin had gone to the kitchen to check the orders for lunch.

'Four, I think,' she replied.

'Do you know St Ives?'

'Not yet - I've only just arrived. But it looks nice.'

'Care to meet me on the beach - say - about five? It's a good place to start.' He had visions of her in a bikini but chastised himself inwardly at the thought of turning into another Larkin. Heaven forbid!

'I'm not...' She hesitated. She didn't have an excuse ready.

'Come on,' he broke in before she had time to come up with one, 'you can't go round looking pale like that - you look as if you're really in need of some rays.'

'I hardly...'

'...know me? What have the last three hours been about, then?'

That was it. Her smile said it all.

'Ok, then. Five o'clock - but which beach? Where...?'

'Porthminster. It's closest to the hotel. I'll be already there, on the beach, right opposite. See you at five.'

Without waiting for her to change her mind he left. *'Five o'clock,'* he thought, *'that gives me four hours to get some sleep.'* Only then did he realised how tired he was.

It was also time for him to take his medication.

He carried them with him at all times. Sometimes his body *told him* when he needed the tablets. He couldn't remember what they were called let alone pronounce their name, nor recall what the consultant had told him his condition was. All he knew was that medication would extend his time on earth and provide him with a quality of life in the process. He could continue to work, as long as it wasn't *too* strenuous. It was why he'd quit his job in the building trade.

'Goodbye bricklaying; hello hospitality industry.'

He also set himself routines to go alongside his course of medication. Normally he would be in bed by nine - A.M. - grab some shut-eye until three in the afternoon, then get up and relax until his shift started at ten - P.M.

Six days a week.

But today was different.

She was different - a reason for changing his routine. Putting in the extra hours for Chef - and then for Larkin - had already unbalanced his day. Now this wonderful new girl had come into his life and he was ready to face any change whatsoever - just to get to know her.

Why not? What else did he have going for him?

Maybe she would add the purpose to his life that had been lacking ever since his diagnosis.

That had been six months ago.

Chapter Two

His alarm was set for four thirty but he'd ignored it until ten to five came and he *did* shake himself awake, and in a panic when he remembered his date with Toni.

'*Yes. It is - it's a date, I guess.*' He was having another conversation with himself as he dressed hurriedly - just shorts and a T-Shirt. He grabbed a towel as he flew out the door and down the steps from his 'digs' - one room and a shared bathroom in a terraced house on Trelawney Avenue.

He ran. *Boy did he run!*

Luckily it was downhill all the way, down the main road into town before cutting through to Tregenna and, finally, crossing the road just up from the station and the steps down to the beach.

It was five minutes past five...and she wasn't there.

He went back up the steps to gain some height so he could scan the beach for her, just in case she had decided to move down to the edge of the water.

Still no sign of her.

'*You've blown it,*' he hissed under his breath, but still audible to passers-by, '*you're such an asshole.*'

'Charming! I know I'm late, but that hardly calls for such insults.' He turned round and...

There she was.

'No - no - *sorry,*' he spluttered. 'It's *me!*'

'I can see it's you, Jake.' Those blue eyes of hers, normally so soft, looked stern. Unforgiving.

'No. It's *me* that's an a-hole,' he explained.

He moderated his expletive this time.

'Apology accepted. But I thought you'd forgotten - or even stood me up. A girl doesn't appreciate being...'

'Yes. I'm so sorry,' he interrupted her yet again. 'I just over-slept,' he explained. 'I haven't had any proper sleep for over twenty hours....it won't happen again.'

'Promise?'

'Yes. I promise.'

'A bit presumptuous, don't you think?'

'Presumptuous.?'

'...that there *will* be a next time.'

She laughed, followed by, 'Just kidding.'

His relief was almost visible. Generally, *he* was used to having the upper hand due to his being taller than most and - as a rule - adopting an air of confidence. Superiority.

But with this girl?

Already she seemed to have the measure of him.

She proved it even further. 'This way,' she beckoned as she led him down across the soft warm sand towards the water's edge, 'I left my towel down here.' It was easy to see.

It read '*St Ives Bay Hotel*'.

'Good move,' he said, congratulating her,

'nobody's going to steal it - they'd be seen a mile away.'

'Snap.' He laid his own hotel towel next to hers. She spread out on her stomach, handing him the bottle with her hand behind her back, fishing for *his* hand.

'Do my back, please?'

She certainly was pale and, although it was late afternoon, the May sunshine was still capable of burning. He took to the task with relish, happy that she seemed easy in his company - so easy in fact, that she trusted him with what could be considered an intimacy shared only with couples who'd known each other much longer.

Longer than a few hours, at least.

He took his time, lingering over every part of her back and shoulders, working the white cream into her skin. He was soon lost. He moved slowly and methodically down towards...

'I'll take over,' she said, retrieving the bottle. She sat up. She'd sensed hesitation in Jake's application of the cream just after he'd finished the small of her back. *'Surely he's not going to carry on down my legs?'* she thought.

She would have been right. He *was* lost - but not *that* lost!

He was just about to pour more cream into his palm and, even without thinking, work the cream into her calves until...who knows *where* it would end? Her sudden movement snapped him out of his trance. She took over by stroking the cream into her lower legs, up over her knees and her lower thighs before she spoke again.

'Do you always stare at people when they're...?'

'Uh...no...,' he spluttered, blushing again as if he'd been caught out - which he had been. 'I was just thinking how you need a few more sessions in the sun so you don't need the cream any more.

'..the next time.'

She smiled - in disbelief.

Her answer was brief. Curt.

'Yeah, right.' She laid back down. 'The *next* time.'

She was the kind of girl who'd become used to attention - and not always welcome attention. Her response, therefore, was natural and automatic for her - to be on her guard. Defensive and to stop 'things' before they went too far. Despite that, and perhaps because she felt Jake was just being normal in many ways, she gradually relaxed.

'I'm sorry,' she added after a brief pause. 'I guess I'm just over-reacting after the day spent with that Larkin chap.'

Jake knew what she was thinking. 'He's just...'

'...a sleaze,' she added.

He lay down next to her, pleased that she was facing inwards so *he* could face *her*. She had her eyes closed, offering him the chance to study her unobserved. Her blonde hair partially hid her face but he could just make out tiny freckles below her eyes, round her nose. Her lips were slightly apart, invitingly, as she breathed out through her mouth.

A few short minutes later she was asleep.

They both were.

Jake awoke first.

A young boy running past had inadvertently flicked sand over Jake's back, waking him up with a start. They had dropped their towels onto soft, warm sand just above the tide-line so that, even when the tide did turn, the waves would stop a few feet short from where they lay. That was the plan, anyway. There was very little swell or even breeze, and the gentle sound of waves breaking on the shoreline created a soothing, calming rhythm.

He raised himself to look far out to sea.

Then he looked down at Toni, resisting the temptation to wake her even though he wanted to talk to her. The sky had clouded over causing it to turn chilly. People began to leave the beach. He picked up his T-shirt and lay it carefully over her back as protection against the cooling air. But not carefully enough. She awoke as soon as she felt him kneeling above her.

'What time is it?'

'About half six,' he replied.

'I'm hungry.' She yawned.

It was just the opening he needed.

'We've missed the evening meal at the hotel,' he

said. 'But I know this great little cafe just up from the harbour.'

'My treat,' he added.

'Sounds perfect,' she said, smiling. 'And I've enjoyed our little...'

'Sleep?'

'Yes, I guess that's what it was,' she said, her smile turning to laughter. 'But don't get the wrong idea. I don't normally sleep with guys on the first date.'

'Is that what this is? A date?'

'If you want it to be.' She stopped what she was doing, which was slipping on her sweater and shorts over her bikini. She looked for the reaction on his face; looked for a response, trying to read his mind.

'A date it is, then,' he said. 'Or was...'

They finished dressing and walked along the sandy beach towards the town, eventually joining up with Pednolva Walk until they reached the pier. By that time the sun had put in another appearance to provide at least some welcome warmth against the light on-shore breeze sweeping across from the west of the town. In the few short weeks Jake had lived in St. Ives he was used to the sudden changes to the weather during a typical day.

Right now the two blended in perfectly with holiday makers - those who were arriving back at lodgings before changing for dinner, whether within their hotel or apartment, or in one of the many restaurants and cafe's. Most hotel staff - kitchen and restaurant workers - had already started their evening shifts an hour or so earlier, but Toni and Jake were different.

Toni's duties were not driven by meal times - more by arrival and departure time for guests, whereas Jake, as night porter, was on call between ten at night until eight in the morning. It was a long shift, but he was allowed a break half way through, during which he tended to have a breakfast, of sorts.

That afternoon they'd missed the evening meal in the staff room, otherwise a breakfast, lunch, and tea were provided as part of their 'wages' - along with free accommodation. That ensured that the low weekly wages - usually between eight and ten pounds depending on rank - represented 'a living wage'.

'Here we are,' said Jake as they arrived at the small bistro tucked away in a narrow backstreet.

By small, it was perhaps twenty feet from door to the kitchen, and by twelve or fourteen at its widest. There were two rows of tables with a mix of two covers and four covers per table which could be pushed together if needed for a party of six. Jake elected for the table by the window, pulling the chair out for Toni before sitting down himself.

He handed her the menu.

'Choose what you want,' he said. 'My treat.'

Toni was glad he'd selected a modest cafe rather

than some swanky restaurant but, then again, they weren't dressed for anything else.

It was spotlessly clean.

'Hi Jake. Good to see you again.' After a respectful delay David, one of the owners, came over and greeted Jake warmly and to take their order.

'Spag Bol, for me,' said Toni. 'And a pot of tea, please.'

'Make that two,' Jake added. He was more interested in Toni rather than what they were going to eat.

In fact, he wasn't even hungry.

Was it nerves?

'Before you ask, they're an item,' said Jake, eager to keep the conversation going, but wondering why he'd decided on such a strange topic; namely the owners of the cafe.

'What...?'

'David...and Gary - the guys that run this place. Own it.'

'Oh,' she said at last, having twigged what Jake was referring to; *the relationship* of David, the waiter, and Gary, the chef. 'I hadn't given it any thought.'

'Sorry, I shouldn't have brought it up.' He hadn't meant to pick on such a topic, but the nerves had kicked in. It's what happens when you are so keen to make an impression - *a good impression* - that you end up risking the opposite.

'It's OK, really.' She was coming to his rescue. Thankfully. 'It is the seventies after all. And St Ives.'

She was, of course, referring to the open-mindedness of the community - influenced by the artist fraternity that had built up over the last few decades, introducing more liberal views.

And then there were the 'townies' - those who'd quit their well-paying jobs and lavish lifestyles in places like London to 'do anything' and/or live off their 'fat', which stretched much further in Cornwall with their cheaper housing and lower cost of living.

But how long would that last once new residents from up country came with their new money, buying up housing and rental opportunities, pushing prices up and beyond the reach of the locals?'

For now those threats to a simple Cornish way of life remained dormant, latent or, at least conveniently ignored.

With all due credit to the locals - those whose links went back generations - they, too, adopted a fairly generous spirit in the acceptance of the non-Cornish 'infiltration' (some would call it), to which they'd been subject since before the war.

Woodstock had happened a few years before, then The Isle of Wight Festival; the hippy generation were opening up not only their own eyes, but causing others to embrace the mood of change. A new liberalism was in the air, and St Ives was just one place where it was breathed in with enthusiasm.

Chapter Three

During the conversation that followed, one that took on a more conventional path, he learnt that Toni came from Harlow. She was escaping the predictable routine of a 'new town' for somewhere she could meet a *mix* of people from different backgrounds. She wanted variety and had heard that such places - like St Ives - could allow her to discover who she really was.

That particular person - who she couldn't say who it *might* be - was not the passenger who sat next to her on the bus home each day, nor any of those with whom she worked in the office at the biscuit factory, nor any of her neighbours. They all seemed resigned to the options limited to within a five mile radius of whatever they called home.

She explained this to Jake and that she wanted more, how she'd immersed herself in literature and been influenced by films and their stars - like Katherine Ross in 'Butch Cassidy' and 'The Graduate', or the 'hippie chicks' in 'Easy Rider' and 'Woodstock'.

She wanted *some* of that life or, at least, the unpredictability it offered - experiences unrestricted by parents, BBC News protocol and The Establishment.

Her other influence had been her best friend Cindy. *She* had left home at Easter to a position she'd seen advertised - a receptionist in another hotel not far from 'The Bay'. 'Mr Roberts' was a boutique establishment where multi-tasking and flexibility were key. Cindy had called Toni about the job in 'The Bay', which *she* had heard through the network and unofficial employment exchange that operated every evening in 'The Lifeboat' pub.

'So. What's *your* story, Jake?' she asked as she finished the last mouthful of spaghetti. 'What're you hiding from?'

The insinuation - accusation, even - took him aback at first. It was uncanny that she had asked 'what' first rather than 'who' he was hiding from, almost as if she'd sensed there had been some 'event' in his past life that had triggered his escape to Cornwall. She'd struck a nerve, noticing how he seemed unsettled by the question. If that wasn't enough, his hesitancy only made her more earnest; more curious.

She pressed him for details.

'Come on, Jake. Give. We're all running from something.'

Over the course of the meal he'd become more relaxed, but now his composure disintegrated.

'Nothing.' He tried to mask his irritation with a muffled laugh, making light of her inquisition. 'I just ended up here in St Ives after...'

He wanted to tell her, but he didn't want to blow it. How would she take what he'd done, the secret only a few knew about, and what he was about to disclose?

'After what?' Her eyes were locked into his, with

a look that insisted - no, *demanded* - he gave her a straight answer.

'...after I got into...'

His inability, *his unwillingness*, to complete the sentence irritated her more.

'Come on. Into what? Into a hot bath? Into debt? Into the wide blue yonder? You're not married, are you? Did you murder someone? Or what?'

'No....well, not quite...'

It wasn't the answer she expected. Not quite...what?

He hesitated again but this time she resisted badgering him for answers. She knew when to back off, eventually adopting a gentler tone.

She gave him the space he needed. *When* he needed it.

In a low voice she apologised, 'Take your time, Jake. It's OK.' Noticing his lack of composure was deepening to an extent where he was having to control his emotions, she caught hold of his hand, realising what was happening. He was returning to a dark place - a place to which she had, just a few moments ago, driven him. Now *she* felt sorry. Guilty.

But she still wanted answers.

Jake finally spoke again, almost choking on his words but managing to hold it together, conscious they were in a public place; trying his best not to draw attention to them.

He hadn't revealed the detail of any of what he

was about to confess - not to anyone apart from his family.

He took a deep breath. She waited. 'Nobody was supposed to be there, let alone die,' he began, in a whisper.

'Where?' she asked - gently - not insisting.

At that point she drew back, having leaned forward over the table and closer to Jake to keep their conversation private. Half of her wasn't sure she did want to hear any more, but Jake carried on, his words still barely audible.

'We got drunk. My mates and me. We'd gone into Erdington for a few drinks - a few too many as it turned out - when one of the chaps, I think it was Charlie, asked who wanted another drink. Anyway, that doesn't matter now; we ended up breaking into The British Legion club. It was on the way home and after midnight, all the lights were off in the club so we all said, "Why not?".

'I was the look-out, outside on the street in case some copper happened by on his night patrol. Meanwhile, Charlie and the other two scaled the back wall and broke in by the rear door. There was no alarm.

'But what we hadn't reckoned on were the old couple asleep in the upstairs flat. They'd heard the sound of breaking glass and come down in time to see Charlie and the boys helping themselves to bottles of whisky - and crisps. We were starving by that time. He started shouting blue murder. His wife began screaming upstairs, threatening to call the police. Charlie and the boys decided to scarper.

'The old boy - he must have been in his seventies - made to come after us but, before he could grab hold of Charlie, he collapsed. Heart attack, apparently.'

Jake paused at that point, turning to Toni to gauge her reaction, surprised that she was still listening to him.

'And you got the blame.'

'For the break-in, yes. Along with all the others. I forget what they were charged with but it wasn't murder - nor manslaughter - because...because it wasn't. It was an accident; sort of. But his death happened while we were committing a crime and the boys were put away.

'I was only look-out so I only got a suspended sentence and a fine. But it nearly killed my mum and dad. That's when I left to come down here. To get away; to make a fresh start.'

'...and to earn enough to pay off your fine, I guess.'

The fact she was still there, next to him and listening, was a total relief. Even though it was the last thing he wanted to reveal about himself, his past shame, he now felt a huge burden lift. He'd finally spoken about that tragic night to someone, at last, after months of bottling it up. More than that, he had told the story *to her* - to Toni - the one who, even in the few short hours since they'd first met, would have been the greatest loss to him if she *had* taken the news badly.

If she'd got up and left.

She hadn't left, but he'd still lied. Not told the full story. There were still some things he had to keep to himself.

Normally he would have been given a custodial sentence too, just like Charlie and the boys. However, the medical report to the court following his recent diagnosis changed all that. His defence had argued - successfully - that prison could pose a serious threat to his life.

On reflection he was already in a prison of a different kind but, since sharing his guilt with Toni he immediately felt better, even though it didn't bring back the life of the old guy who'd died at the scene of his crime.

He was put on probation following the suspended sentence, reporting every week to his case officer and given a monthly plan to pay off his fine.

Jake had missed that part out to Toni, the part where his health condition had saved him from jail. He wasn't ready to open up about that - just yet. Maybe he never would. The less complicated things were, the better. His criminal past was quite enough to own up to so soon into their relationship - if there was to be any relationship after today. He needed at least some clues - from Toni - on that subject.

'You don't mind, then?' he asked after a while.

'No...well, yes, of course I mind,' she replied. 'It's not something I'm used to, knowing someone who...'

She paused, about to say 'is a criminal.' Instead she simply said, 'Let's just take one step at a time, can we?'

It was the best he could hope for, he figured. It was too early. She needed space to process the information that had hit her sideways; that would have derailed most people. The last thing she needed at this time was to be pressured for a reaction; a verdict. A judgement. That would come later, perhaps. or not at all. Her immediate response was cheerful, positive. Her eyes said more than her words.

'Thanks. Yes. That'd be great.' He was relieved she hadn't walked out the door and never wanted to talk to him again. But she respected his honesty, glad that he'd decided to tell her rather than keep it from her; something as serious as being involved in someone's death even if it wasn't his fault.

'I had a nice time,' she said as she rose to go. She'd delayed her exit until it seemed the right moment and couldn't be taken as a reaction to his revelation. An escape. 'If you don't mind, I'll head back to the hotel. I've had a long day.'

'Me too,' he replied. 'I'm back on shift in a couple of hours; at ten. I might grab an hour's shut-eye first.'

They walked back to the main street. 'No need to take me the rest of the way,' she said. The hotel was along the road to the left whereas Jake's place was up the hill to the right. It was still light with plenty of people about, so he agreed.

She'd be safe enough.

He kissed her cheek softly. 'See you tomorrow,' They went their separate ways. 'I had a nice time too.'

Toni's thoughts were filled with what Jake had just admitted to her; that he had a record. But, for some reason it didn't seem to matter - not influencing how she felt towards him. Not in a bad way. She still felt safe around him but she had no idea why that was. And the fact he'd shared a secret with her - so soon after they had just met, only hours before - gave a her a sense of confidence.

Confidence in Jake. Trust.

Her only worry now was her own situation, one that she felt she *ought* to share with him; *to be honest* with him in the way he'd been with her. Especially now. But *was* it the right time? Was it too soon? After all, as far as she knew he might wake up a day or two later and decide he didn't want anything to do with her. They'd only known each other, literally, hours.

But they'd walked away from each other each still bearing a secret; a secret from each other...

Chapter Four

Toni had a car.

Even on the meagre hotel wages, bearing in mind the free lodgings and free meals, her finances worked out OK. With few additional outgoings and the frugal culture and lifestyle she'd adopted - spiritual rather than material - there were no other real demands on her cash flow.

It was now two weeks since they'd first met. They'd agreed from the outset to 'take things as they come'; but, in their case that meant things moved fast.

They couldn't help themselves.

As difficult as it could be working at the same hotel, their shift patterns meant they had *some* shared time - at work and off duty - whilst enjoying enough time apart so they could *then* appreciate their time together.

Also in their favour was that Larkin didn't bother Toni. At least not in *that* way. He had Jake 'on his radar' so he timed his own day off to coincide with Jake's. The upside of that was that Jake would always be around just in case Larkin *did* try it on with Toni if Jake wasn't around. The downside was that Jake didn't enjoy the luxury of a day at work *without* Larkin looking over his shoulder - *to check everything 'he got up to'* in Larkin's words.

Toni also made sure she shared the same day off as

Jake - which they really *did* share. Toni had her own 'live-in' deal as part of her employment package - her own room on the top floor of the hotel. That meant they took every opportunity to be together - including a delicious lie-in on their days off. It was also a day minus any intrusion from Larkin, given that he spent *his* days off with his wife and family in Newquay.

Could it possibly all work out better for them?

Fortunately - or unfortunately, if you happened to be a chamber-maid in the hotel - there were other distractions to keep Larkin busy 'in that way'. With Toni and Jake quite open that they were seeing each other, that in itself was enough reason for Larkin to keep his distance. He was also privy to Jake's criminal record. His past, plus his size, was sufficient disincentive for Larkin to cross the line.

Larkin had heard about the death at the crime scene.

Jake realised meeting Toni was a big turning point for him. He was pondering that very notion as he headed down to the hotel after his day's sleep - that it counted as his official 'bed-time' - to meet her after *her* shift ended at five o'clock.

They'd arranged to go for an evening drive.

Botallack was a disused mine some twelve miles from St Ives. They took the coastal road so they could enjoy the evening sunset. It was a slow road - taking about half an hour - but they were in no hurry.

Jake wasn't due on until ten and Toni wasn't a fast driver anyway.

'Plenty of places to park,' said Jake, stating the obvious as soon as they arrived. It was a quiet time. Remoteness and the chance to explore more of Cornwall away from the business of St Ives was what they were after.

They weren't disappointed. The stillness and calm, with nobody else in sight, was just what they wanted. Its peacefulness wafted over them like a spell, providing a perfect time to think. Toni had been quiet most of the journey, concentrating on the road ahead - or so Jake told himself. But she had other things on her mind. The emptiness of their surroundings, despite the fact that it was rich in natural beauty with breathtaking views out to sea, helped Toni process her inner thoughts. It wasn't until they'd begun their walk along the cliff that she broke her silence.

'Are you afraid of dying, Jake?'

Woa, where did that come from? he mused.

They'd been tracing the coastal path where it was wide enough for them to walk side-by-side, when this unusual question came from nowhere. Jake was used to some surprises from Toni, that's what he loved about her. She was never boring and sparked in him realisations that there were things, and things to think about to consider, beyond his own universe. But the darkness of her words, and a mood that seemed to match the grey clouds on the horizon, told him this was something different. Even for her.

The clouds were born on an onshore breeze - typical of the north coast - gathering pace and threatening rain within the next ten minutes. Now his thoughts were not so much on the weather, but on Toni. What was going on?

'I haven't thought about it,' he replied. 'Why do you ask?'

She didn't answer straight away. 'And why now?' he pressed her. She was quicker to answer this time.

'I was just thinking about what you must have gone through - seeing that old guy collapse and die right there and then in front of you when you broke into the British Legion.

'What did you *feel*?'

'Shock, mainly. But afterwards regret. I couldn't help but feel sorry for his wife. It's those left behind that carry the burden of dying.'

'Death? It's a burden?'

'It is for those you leave behind.'

'What if you knew *you* were dying? How d'you think *that* would feel?'

'You get used to it.'

'Sounds like you know, Jake.' She paused, waiting for the confirmation that never came. She pressed him again. Did she sense he'd stopped just short of really opening again?

'Well - *do* you?'

'I...errr...I'm just guessing.' Should he remain in

denial of his own condition, or come clean?

She blocked the way ahead for him by confronting him face on. 'You *would* tell me, *wouldn't you*, Jake?'

'Tell you what?'

'If ever you...if ever you needed to - to tell me anything I *ought* to know. Like you did with that break-in thing.'

He didn't answer but it did leave him wondering if she'd picked up on something - as if she had some 'sixth sense' - or, at least, that she knew there was something he wasn't telling her. He turned the question over in his own mind and wondered whether to say more until...the moment passed.

He'd left it too late to provide *any* answer - yes *or* no. She was moving ahead again - literally as well as in her thoughts - walking at quite a pace and ahead of him in single file. But she kept her head down. It was like a cloud had descended over them both. When she took a tissue from her jeans pocket and brought it up to her face, he knew something wasn't right.

He called out. 'Hold on, will you?'

She stopped, but still faced ahead.

'What is it, Toni? What's wrong?' He placed his hands gently on her shoulders making her face *him*, not surprised to see tears streaming down her face.

'I'm *so* sorry,' she began. 'I love you so much and couldn't bear to be without you.'

'I'm not going anywhere.' He drew her close as he lied.

'No. Not you. Me. I might...' She pulled away slightly, raising her eyes first, then her head, fully meeting his gaze.

'*I* might be going.'

'Don't say that. I won't *let* you go.'

He held her even closer.

'You don't understand,' she choked, unable to explain further until, finally, his warmth and comforting arms settled her.

'Jake, I have this...this sickness inside me that might take me. Take me away from you. I've had it for some time now but recently it's been getting worse. The doctors give me stuff to control it, but they said I needed to get away to the coast or somewhere. The countryside, or where the air is cleaner.'

It was her confession time: 'That's why I'm really here.'

The idea of losing her gradually sank in - the gravity of it - but all he could do, all he could *think* of doing, was to hold her. Hold her for fear that she *would* escape him.

'Not today, please,' he whispered, 'and not tomorrow, nor the next day...'

'Never.'

The secret she'd now shared had only just hit him when he thought about his own situation, his own recent diagnosis and the fact that *he* had no guarantees either as to how long *he* would survive. He might be lucky and last years - after all there were always new drugs for rare illnesses. But until he'd met Toni it somehow hadn't seemed important. Not to him.

He hadn't really cared how long it might be until...

Now things were different, even more so after she'd dropped this bombshell and, with it came a new responsibility. How could he leave her to cope with *his* loss - with hers to come perhaps soon after - to face alone? How could he be so selfish? But he was glad she had such faith - enough to trust in him and share her most innermost secret.

Two secrets in fact.

The second was admitting she really did love him.

He made up his mind in an instant. He would live.

He would live to see it through. Live in spite of himself and to see it through to the end. To outlive *her*. In no way was she going to live *just one minute* without *him*.

But should he admit how ill *he* was?

They sat on the cliff edge facing the lowering sun, it's warmth bathing their faces. The threat of a shower had decided to miss them after all. Instead the gloom of the grey rain-clouds covered the headland north of them, always retreating, sheets of falling rain just visible, more of a mist sweeping across the surface as it faded into the distance.

A rainbow arched overhead from land to sea.

Perhaps it was a sign.

'I'm glad you told me,' he said finally, drawing her closer into his chest with a comforting arm. 'It means a lot to me.'

He didn't have to explain why, even though a momentary shiver coursing through him, nearly gave him away. He kept it that way, the fear kept inside whilst outside he remained relatively calm. He had to - he *owed* it to her. She would never find out - not *from* him nor *about* him - because *she didn't need to know*. If she really was only going to live months rather than years - hopefully many years - he was determined they would be the happiest days of her life.

And of *his* life.

Apart from that one fact - *his* life prospects - it was just another case of being totally open and honest with each other. At least that's how it felt between them at that moment. But his non-disclosure didn't make Jake feel any better about himself. He was still holding back from her just as she was laying herself open emotionally, before him.

But what was he to do? She needed his strength right now, an assurance in her own mind that he would be there for her should she ever need to intensify her treatment, or cope with going into remission. For him now, so very soon after her admitting her illness to him, for him to weigh in with his own health issues would be just wrong. Selfish.

Cruel.

For all *those* reasons he needed her not to know.

It was best if he carried the weight of his own secret purely by himself; of that he was certain. He had his medication; he had his routines; he had a life-style allowing him to cope with the uncertainty with which his own condition presented him.

Most of all he had Toni. *She* was now his purpose.

She'd entered his life at exactly the right time. The new strength she'd given *him* - the confidence and faith that life was worth living after all - gave *him* strength. It was a trade-off ensuring he was fully equipped to support *her*.

With the threat of the squall past they continued on their walk at a more leisurely pace. They'd found a map describing a circular route along the coastal path, before turning to cut across open fields, then back to the car. Meanwhile, they were both lost in thought and barely spoke until features of the disused mine ruins came into view. For Jake, one burning question still needed to be answered.

'Why did you decide to tell me now?'

It didn;t take her long to answer.

'I needed to be certain - about you, I mean - and the growing feeling that I really *know* you gave me the chance, gave me the courage...'

'The same way you've inspired me, I suppose, ever since I first met you,' he said, 'and from that first day in the cafe.'

She felt the same.

'Normally, hearing someone had a criminal record would have scared me,' she said. 'But somehow - perhaps *the way* you told me and so soon after we'd met - it meant so much more to me.

'I never had any doubts after that,' she added.

He laughed. 'My only doubt about you was whether or not you'd turn up on that first day.'

'Really?'

'Well, I was a bit pushy as I recall. I was worried I might be pressurising you. Forcing you to...'

'I'm glad you did,' she grinned. 'In fact, I was hoping you would ask. Didn't you guess?'

'Ha! I thought you might be above my pay grade,' he admitted. 'I didn't think you'd be interested in an ex-brickie!'

She looked disappointed. 'So you thought I was shallow then? Stuck up?'

'Not really,' he said. 'I just couldn't believe my luck.' It was the right compliment to end the conversation, but she still needed one final assurance.

'You won't tell anyone else, will you?' she whispered as he slid into the passenger seat next to her.

'Larkin doesn't even know.'

Chapter Five

One year later...the day of the funeral.

Jake sat alone on the bench in the back garden of Toni's parents' house in Winchester.

Alone with his thoughts. She was gone.

But for the past year he and Toni had achieved what they'd pledged - one they'd made to each other as the day drew to a close on their return from Botallack.

He remembered it with fondness now, recalling how the setting sun bathed her blonde curls in such a way they appeared golden - strands of pure gold massing into curls with an abandon matching the freedom with which she found herself after sharing the burden of her illness with him.

The sun was low but with at least an hour to go before it sank beyond the horizon - below the perfect straight line of the Atlantic Ocean at its furthermost point. Soon there would be an intense pathway of golden light, a rich ocean carpet reaching out towards them, almost enticing them to take those first tentative steps onto it, to a point into the unknown.

Their unknown future. A turning point.

'It's almost as if you could walk straight from the shore and as far as where it reaches the sky,' she'd said, sensing what he was thinking, reading his thoughts. Again.

He turned from the cliff top and to her, despite the sun's rays having almost blinded him. She was already facing him even though she was driving. Her eyes met his, albeit briefly, due to the narrowness of the road. As the next bend approached she was forced to concentrate - on driving.

As he recalled that very instant, now, he'd marvelled at how much bluer they'd become, not so long after she had shared her secret with him.

They'd become brighter.

Their natural colour was soft but, in comparison to now, had seemed dull due to her spending most of her time indoors back home in Harlow. Over recent weeks they'd changed, taking on a radiance of their own. Time together shared on the beach, or on walks along the cliffs beyond Clodgy Point, always outside in the open air whenever they had a chance, had given her eyes a much deeper colour and brilliance.

It equalled her new joy and optimism.

To Jake, that extra sparkle in her eyes was proof that he was fulfilling his promise to her that life would take on new meaning, purpose and richness - everything she deserved.

And, *why* did she deserve this?

Because every lift in her spirit repaid him several fold. He looked forward to and relished every new day with Toni. His pledge to support and take care of her meant that he, too, now cared about living again. But the real bonus, for him, was that this new responsibility had an honesty and sincerity all of its own; it was more than just a duty. Much more.

It was born out of a deep love.

Those merciful, loving hours - times when neither of them ever contemplated that the sheer exhilaration of waking up in the morning and taking that first breath - could get much better, reached a new significance by the close of that summer. The whole balance of life had changed and was about to change even more.

He remembered the phone call. Toni was just finishing her hotel shift at five o'clock when it came through to Reception.

It was her mother.

'I have some good news,' her mother declared.

'Me too,' Toni replied.

'Me first.'

'Oh, go on, Mum. What is it?'

The line went silent. Toni couldn't make out what the muffled sound was at the other end. Was it laughter? Crying?

Or a mixture of both?

'Mum? What is it? What's going on?'

Still no words from her mother, until, 'We've had a bit of luck on the pools.'

'The football pools?'

'Yes. The Treble Chance. Horace Bachelor.'

'Horace...?'

'Oh, it doesn't matter, Toni. We're rich! Your

dad's won thousands. We can afford to retire.'

'Mum? It's only five o'clock. Have you been...?'

'Just a couple of glasses of sherry. We're allowed to celebrate, aren't we?'

'Well, yes, I suppose...'

'Suppose nothing. Here's your father, anyway.'

'Dad?'

'Hello, darling.' Her father's tone was calmer, but she could still sense an excitement that was hard to fully contain.

'Is it true?'

'You bet it's true. No more getting up at four in the morning for my early shift at the Post Office. I quit!' With that he laughed, half in relief but mostly out of pure joy.

'That's wonderful news, dad.'

He became calm again. 'Anyway, what's your news?'

Toni cleared her throat, controlling her own emotions was a little difficult now. '*Here goes,*' she thought, then...

'Jake and I are getting engaged.'

Her parents were ecstatic, much to her delight and to Jake's relief. They felt they'd won the football pools twice over. Their dreams had come true. They - George and Margaret - could escape Harlow and move closer to Margaret's twin sister in Winchester, buying a large family home with a large garden they could both enjoy in retirement.

But it was a celebration that proved short-lived. By the following spring it was clear to them, and confirmed by specialists, that Toni's new-found health and vigour would be short-lived. As the previous autumn turned into winter, and the harshness of the short January days bit hard, her whole demeanour seemed to suffer. Despite the new joy she had found with Jake, coupled with the healthy climate and lifestyle in St Ives, her medication was fighting a losing battle.

Was it the fact that she and Jake could no longer spend precious evening hours relaxing on the beach between shifts, or watch the surfers catch the final waves of the day on Porthmeor Beach, or perhaps it was the lack of fresh sea air? Whatever the reason, the results back from her latest tests and the diagnosis from her specialist were conclusive.

She wouldn't see another summer.

Toni's parents *had* taken their planned early retirement and moved to Winchester. Her aunt lived in the town and her mum had always wanted to be reunited closer to her twin. It was a large four bedroom detached house in a semi-rural location with the larger garden her dad had always wanted. Jake and Toni had taken up their offer 'to winter over' in Winchester with them.

Now there was a double necessity to do so. It would be where Toni was to spend her final days. Jake was at her bedside for her final hours until she slipped away.

'The cars have arrived.'

It was the day of the funeral. Margaret found Jake he was finishing the last of his coffee. He needed moments on his own before the funeral cars came but now he rose as he heard them crunching on the gravel driveway at the front of the house.

'I'm ready.' He took her arm.

Toni's father joined them as they moved slowly and reverently towards the sleek, black stretch limousines.

'Faith isn't here, George?'

'Not yet, Margaret,' her husband answered.

The brief interchange left Jake mildly curious. He'd not heard the name mentioned before but he soon forgot about it; dismissed it. His concern now was his final goodbye to Toni.

There was no 'Faith' at the crematorium and they never mentioned the name again.

Chapter Six

Another six months went by...

With Toni now gone, Jake returned to The St Ives Bay Hotel, but not to his old job. The consortium that had taken over the hotel in close season were progressive and believed in succession management. He was on a training programme and promoted to assistant manager.

Larkin was gone, leaving under a cloud after some misconduct involving one of the maids - that, or his wife found out about his dalliances and he went back to Newquay and his family to try to mend the damage.

Jake didn't really care about the 'hows and whys'.

And that was the double tragedy.

He accepted his new responsibilities with sufficient energy and enthusiasm to tick all the boxes when it came to his reviews and assessments. Otherwise, it was very much a case of going through the motions. He looked after his staff well and, to that extent, he *did* care - but his underlying attitude was functional rather than personal.

It was enough.

The hotel went through close season refurbishments and the first thing he addressed was the Lobby and the Reception where Toni had spent most of her time. Staff appointments were his responsibility, including the hiring of a new receptionist for the start of the new season. Toni had been a trainee. This time he decided on a fully qualified candidate - mature in years and experience - and male.

He couldn't risk any memories of Toni affecting his ability to function and wanted no distractions, shutting down any opportunity, where possible, for old memories to emerge. But, if that was really the case, surely he would have chosen a new place to work, a new location, even a new line of work. Although he wouldn't admit it, even to himself, he was still hanging on to memories of Toni and their life together.

Why wouldn't he? She was the love of his life.

His excuse would have been, and unconsciously without really being rationally thought through, that he needed to preserve existing foundations to get him through this. Going back to the building trade wasn't an option given that he was still on maintenance medication for his 'condition'. What else was there? Weighing it all up, retaining parts of his status quo offered the best choice.

He included monthly trips to Toni's parents as part of that 'need to stay connected' to elements from his life with Toni.

'Could I add a few more days onto my weekend this month, Patron? If that's OK.'

He was asking Carlos, one of the Spanish managers drafted in to strengthen the level of hotel group expertise.

'How long do you need, Jake?'

'Five days at the most.'

'Dare I ask if there's any special reason for... 'mas dias de vacaciones'... this.... extra leave?'

'It's a year since I lost my...' He couldn't finish.

'Esta bien, por supuesto que puedes. Take as long as you need - dentro de lo razonable...within reason.'

'Thank you.' Jake's reply was barely audible, but he gave a weak smile and a nod as he left the office.

It was lunch-time when he arrived in Winchester a week later. He made most of the journey by train.

'Come here my boy,' gushed Margaret as he walked up the drive to Toni's parents' house. She'd been weeding the roses in the front garden when the taxi drew up, half expecting it to be him.

Toni's dad, George, joined them from the rear of the house where he'd been feeding the compost heap, joining them for a group hug. He also missed the boy, who he treated as a son and all the more now, acknowledging the gravity of the anniversary.

'How are you, Jake?'

George's question was unnecessary. He could see how Jake felt by the look on his face. Drawn. Fighting back tears he embraced George, holding on as if his life depended on it.

In a way it did.

Without George and Margaret who else did he

have - flesh and blood - to allow him to cling onto those precious days with Toni? If not with him, this was where Toni belonged. There was some talk of Toni's ashes being placed at the St Ives cemetery Barnoon, overlooking Porthmeor Beach - or even scattered in the Atlantic from The Island. But Jake was in a really bad place immediately after Toni passed away. That, as well as his not knowing *where* he might be living and working after the funeral, meant that the most sensible option was to bury her in Winchester, close to her parents.

Margaret also hoped it would mean they would see more of Jake. She was happier having Jake with them, and she loved Winchester now she was close to her twin sister, Joyce.

Jake noticed the change in her.

Were there special reasons she'd wanted to be close to Joyce? It *did* mean Margaret could pay her sister regular visits, although George never went with her; nor had Jake, nor Toni. There were questions that might be answered later but, for now, their thoughts were all with Toni.

They took Jake inside.

'You must be starving. Can I get you a sandwich?' asked Margaret, taking the first opportunity to mother him.

'Thanks, but no, Margaret,' he replied, 'I want to go straight there, if you don't mind.'

"There" was the cemetery where Toni had been

laid to rest.

'Do you want company?' George reached for his coat expecting a 'Yes', but Jake hesitated.

'I'd take that as a "No", George,' Margaret whispered, but Jake heard.

'That's OK - both of you. Thanks. I just need a little time. I'll be gone about an hour.'

'Take my car,' George offered. 'If you want...'

'I prefer to walk. I can feel her - here - near.' The husband and wife looked at each other, understanding, and in a way that they always seemed to agree with each other. They still felt it too, despite Toni having only lived with them *in that house* for a matter of months. Jake left them to fix their own lunch, offering a brief wave before setting out for the churchyard where Toni lay.

It was some fifteen minutes' walk away.

Gazing around as he made his way to the churchyard he could feel her. He recalled times and events from the previous year before she died, and how happy they both were - staying with her parents for that first winter after the season ended. Jake found temporary work in the Post Office thanks to George's connections. Christmas meant they were taking on extra staff for deliveries.

But as the New Year arrived it became apparent that Toni was failing, though she did her best not to make it obvious to those around her. Jake sensed it first, which was a blessing. It meant the doctors, and the medication that they increased in response to her deterioration, dulled the pain and gave her a better 'quality of life', as they called it - even though her usual zest for fun was dulled.

And she could see the pain - her pain - in Jake.

Chapter Seven

Her final hours, and days, were spent in the local hospice. It was one where loved ones could stay too, so that final memories for both could be shared - and even enjoyed, if that were possible. He and Toni even joked about Larkin - the sleaze - and what her time at The Bay might have been like were it not for Jake. They agreed that nothing would have been as good, as happy and as full, were it not for each other.

Even at the saddest times, like these.

He was reading to her at the time her final moment did come. They were together on the hospice bed, she inside the covers, he on top - but together. He was holding her hand whilst managing to turn the pages with the other. It was her favourite book.

Wuthering Heights.

He continued even though she was slipping in and out of consciousness, muttering some comment to him now and again that he could barely decipher, her attempt to prove she was still listening.

After all, she knew the book virtually off by heart.

He paused as he felt her grip soften, then release him.

She had finally given up. Gone.

The nurse was monitoring her vital signs, remotely, and now entered the room swiftly and silently to check her pulse.

She shook her head. 'I'm so sorry.'

She left the room, and Jake. Alone.

Jake remained beside Toni, shaking uncontrollably but with barely a sound, taking up her hand once more whilst it was still warm. It was his way of clinging on to her last signs of life. It seemed to be growing darker outside. Street lights at the end of the driveway into the hospice grounds were flickering on. He had no idea how long he'd laid there, trying to contain his emotion; but what was the use? He finally let it all out, the sound of his grief causing the nurse to look in, only to close the door silently behind her to return to her desk.

She had seen it so many times before, but still reached for her box of tissues in the desk drawer.

An hour later George and Margaret entered the room where Jake and Toni both lay, still side-by-side.

Margaret panicked. Jake had his eyes closed.

'Jake? Jake? Are you...?'

He opened his eyes. Margaret was overcome with relief, moving over to embrace him as her first thoughts were proven wrong. But if Jake *had* been taken too, would that have been a blessing - at least for him? Little did she realise he'd allowed his eyes to close as a way to cope, to finally come to terms - or perhaps *not* come to terms - with the fact that Toni was gone.

He wished he could join Toni *right now*, just as they'd imagined, hoped, to be with each other even in death.

Because...what was the point without her?

Jake raised himself from the bed, placing his slippered feet on the floor to stand up. Instinctively, Margaret took his arm in case he needed steadying, but he was fine. He was fully clothed and, as loathe as he was to leave Toni's side, decided the decent thing to do was to allow George and Margaret to be with their daughter on their own.

He left the room.

The nurse met Jake, but without saying a word. She knew from so many previous occasions that words, *her* words, would be meaningless. Instead she offered him a glass of water and a couple of tablets, which he took without question.

'I might go for a walk.' He headed for the garden.

Margaret found him seated by the fountain and the pond where so many patients and their most loved ones found peace and solace during visiting hours. And for times like these. She was holding it together remarkably well as she sat next to him, but he barely noticed. She knew that 'her boys', as she called them, both Jake and George, needed her to be strong.

And so she was. Strong for them.

That was a year ago.

Those thoughts faded as he was now approaching the cemetery. The hinges creaked as he pushed open the cast iron gates to the pathway leading through the centre of lines of graves, stones and plaques carrying heart-felt inscriptions. Toni lay - he still instinctively referred to her in his mind in the present tense - in a sunny, south-facing plot next to the small chapel to which the path was leading.

He could see the small headstone ahead, amongst an array of flowers. But who was that figure standing over it?

A shiver - like a ghost - ran through him. She had the same height, figure, bearing and hair colour - as Toni.

Could it be...?

No. He didn't believe in ghosts.

Did he?

He approached cautiously but the figure, a scarf covering most of the bowed head, remained un-moved, appearing not to hear his footsteps on the gravel.

He coughed softly, politely, so as not to startle her.

She turned to face him.

'I'm sorry.' His apology was automatic and unne-cessary; after all what did he have to apologise for?

It wasn't Toni, or at least, it didn't look like Toni.

Not exactly, but there was *something*.

But what?

The sunglasses didn't help.

He decided to introduce himself. 'I'm...'

'Jake. Yes, I know.'

'How do...?'

'I recognise you from the photographs.'

'The...? What...? Who...?'

'The ones my sister sent me.'

He stood frozen, a puzzled look on his face.

'Toni was my sister,' she was taking off her sunglasses as she said it. 'My -'

'- twin sister.' Jake filled in the gap himself. Now he saw the resemblance. It was a close resemblance. They were almost identical. Especially...

'You've got her eyes,' he added.

Now *she* froze - the truth in what he'd said suddenly hit her; astounding her. 'How did you know?'

'Blue. Nobody has eyes *so* blue, apart from...'

She was beginning to understand. 'You really *don't* know, do you? Did you even know about me before?'

'I'm...I'm not sure what you're driving at.' He didn't mean to sound irritated; it was just how it came out. He needed answers not, 'the third degree'.

'Toni never told me about any sister, let alone a twin...'

'She never mentioned a Faith?'

He didn't answer her directly, but it was starting to make sense. George and Margaret *had* mentioned her once, just as they were about to get into the car to the funeral.

He switched from *de*fensive to *off*ensive.

'You didn't make it to the funeral then?'

'I couldn't.' She was clearly upset by the assertion. It was more like an accusation. A reprimand.

'Couldn't? or wouldn't? Didn't bother? Didn't care *about your own sister?*'

He was pushing her too far and he knew it, but he'd bottled up his anger to do with the unfairness of it all, he just needed an excuse to level it at someone. A tear ran down her cheek, escaping from those beautiful, vibrant, blue eyes. It was a familiar blue.

'Couldn't,' she protested. 'I was still recovering from the operation.'

He said nothing. Here was another mystery. Operation? What operation? She spoke as if he should already know - and, perhaps he should have. But he didn't; he hadn't.

What *was* this *operation*?

'My eyes. The transplant. For my eyes. I was having her eyes. She donated them to me. It was her dying wish. You were burying my sister and all the time I was taking her eyes, just one of many brilliant things about her. I didn't deserve it, just as she didn't deserve to die.'

She finished, breaking down into sobs. Now he *did* understand. Of course that's why she - Faith - missed the funeral. How could she? Toni was a donor, which explained why there was a delay in her funeral, but nobody had told him.

Not her parents. And not even Toni.

Why not?

That part he may never know - not unless George and Margaret could shed any light - assuming, that is, they *did* know. One thing was for sure, she had departed this world but she was still proving to be the wonderful person she was, always putting other people first - *giving* herself, even in death.

But how come she was able to donate her eyes to Faith? And why? Was she born blind? How dare he even start that conversation with - with Faith - minutes within meeting her? Coupled with that, his rant hardly endeared him to her.

She made it easy for him.

'I had an accident,' she disclosed. 'But it was my fault.'

'How did it happen?'

She began to explain but, first, she needed to lay the ground so that he would fully understand - not just about her eyes, but why the family had kept it - and her - such a secret.

'They were ashamed of me. Not just mum and dad, my aunt, but Toni as well. Although in some ways she was responsible - but not in a blame-like way, but because of who she was. She was the perfect one whereas, well, I was bad.'

'Bad? How?'

That part he found so hard to take in at first. How could someone so like Toni - good and loved by everyone - be so different from her twin? Bad?

He was soon to find out.

'Look, I know it sounds like an excuse, one that you've heard before, but I got in with the wrong crowd. You see, Toni couldn't go to college or university, partly due to her illness and all the treatment she had to have at first. But I could, and did. It was art school and, you know what it's like, there were drugs. I sort of got hooked, and on the serious stuff.

'That kind of gear cost money so, to afford an expensive habit, my boyfriend and I - he was into it as well - got into the manufacture. Only small scale, in the flat we had. Experimenting. We didn't get any further than that because that's when the accident happened.

'It blew up in my face - quite literally - when we were cooking this stuff. It cost me my eyes, and my family with it. Up to that point my behaviour wasn't exactly - well - exemplary anyway. This was the last straw and they'd already disowned me, even though mum tried to help turn my life round.'

All the time Jake was listening to this he was knelt by Toni's gravestone, imagining how she managed a normal life whilst all this was going on with her twin sister.

He looked up at Faith.

'You can't see any scars.' His was a question more than an observation.

'It's amazing what plastic surgery can do these days,' she replied. 'That's why I look a little different from her. They couldn't make me look exactly how I was, just close enough.'

He looked back at the gravestone, reading the sign-off to the inscription he'd insisted they include, realising how ironic - and, technically, untrue it was.

One of a kind.

'So, Faith, you really *do* have Toni's eyes.'

'Yes, and that's why I missed the funeral. I was just recovering from the operation, which they couldn't rush because there was no guarantee it would be successful. I had to stay in rehabilitation for weeks afterwards, by which time you'd gone back to St. Ives for the season.'

'And your mum and dad still found it hard to accept you back, especially whilst they were getting over the loss of Toni.' said Jake, but speculating. He went on.

'That bit I don't get. If you were so like Toni, and your folks were so distraught when she died, surely having you around would have been a comfort for them.'

'You're only half right, Jake. I'm sorry,' she said. 'Toni was... so perfect... whilst I was the opposite, it would have made things worse.

'They wanted Toni back and I wasn't the answer. Instead I've been living with my aunt across town. I've just had to wait for the time for mum and dad to be ready. Not so much mum, but dad, certainly.'

He was standing now, stood over the gravestone and next to Faith. They remained silent, remembering

Toni, lost in their own thoughts and safe in their own memories.

Separate memories.

Jake was first to break the silence.

'Maybe that time is now.'

'Do you really think so?' Her voice faltered as the idea of finally being reconciled with her parents - the reconnection that she so badly craved - sank in.

'What proof do you need?' he asked.

She took a deep breath. 'I guess I was hoping Toni would provide the answer like she always did when she was... that's why I came here, came here first."

He knew what she meant and unconsciously placed his arm round her shoulder. She leaned into him. It seemed so natural for both of them, forgetting that only ten minutes before they had been strangers. It was an intimacy that neither of them expected or had planned, yet it felt so right. Moments later and after their goodbyes to Toni, they walked back down the gravel path towards the cemetery gates.

Jake opened them to let Faith through first.

Only then did he take his arm from her shoulder.

'I'm sorry.'

It was as if he'd suddenly realised what he'd been doing but didn't want it to be taken the wrong way.

This was his second apology.

Her smile put him at ease. 'You know it's OK.'

'How would I know?' he asked.

'*She* secretly told you it was alright - or would

have - otherwise you wouldn't have comforted me. Not like that.'

'Really?'

'Yes,' she went on. 'In the same way she told me not to worry, not to feel guilty, and to come back with you so I can reconcile things with my mum and dad.'

To that day he'd been wanting a connection of some kind - any kind - with Toni, after her passing. Until that point it had never came. Likewise, he'd never really believed in the idea of people 'speaking to the living from the grave.'

Now maybe... just maybe... he should.

Now maybe... just maybe... she had, and through her own eyes.

~ *** THE END *** ~

You Only Love Once
A short romantic story
J S Morey

First published in Great Britain 2023

Further reading:

The series 'Love should never be this hard':

Book 1: The Sign of the Rose
Book 2: The Black Rose of Blaby
Book 3: Rose: The Missing Years
Book 4: Finding Rose

Wild Hearts Roam Free – and Wild Hearts Come Home
Two modern westerns set in Wyoming

Unresolved? - a short story linked to 'Wild Hearts Roam Free'

Those Italian Girls – set in the hills of Tuscany

Read My Shorts – short stories and poems with a message

Wood-Spirit - an anthology of poems about trees

For more by this author
visit www.newnovel.co.uk

Chapter One

He glanced up to her from where he had fallen.

She was already looking across at him. Hers was a look of curiosity rather than concern.

A chill coursed through his upper body as her eyes penetrated his very being as if she was reaching into his soul. The frantic movement of the game blurred into oblivion; the sound of feet running was muted and the shouts for the soccer ball indistinct.

All he could see was her.

He saw how her form was graceful, well-defined, and the features of her face – that beautiful, perfect face – cast a spell over him, freezing his movements momentarily, detaching him from his surroundings.

The fall he'd taken after the tackle from Carl had sent him flying across the grass but there was no referee's whistle. It was just a friendly kick-about on the local park. The real soccer match was this weekend – Saturday afternoon. It was now Tuesday – Tuesday evening on a warm September. It was still light; the team could train without floodlights.

The park was open to everyone and anyone but he had never seen *her* before. How could *that* be? In all his seventeen years in the village he'd grown to know just about *every*one, if not personally then by sight and by name.

But *this* girl? She was a mystery. And *so* different.

She must be new to the village and from one of the

many families who'd moved into houses on the new estate – the estate built on the fields that had once been his – or, at least his playground during school holidays and weekends.

But he'd moved on from those days.

All that was before he'd started work 'in town', as they used to refer to it. The transition from schoolboy to wage earner had taken place three months ago and explained why he'd not seen her before. She was way more beautiful *in every way* than any of the other village girls and yet he still didn't know her. That would change.

It would *have to* change.

But how?

How *would* he get to know her? (And he really, *really* had to get to know her. He'd made up his mind about that, in an instant.) She looked maybe a year younger than himself, although he had no idea whatsoever how he'd come to that conclusion.

Assuming he was right.

Meanwhile he just lay there feigning injury just so he could remain there looking at her. His fall was cushioned by the lush yet-to-be-mown grass ready for the next game. But he eventually sat up, if only to make it easier for him to get a better look as she continued to walk past him. She was close, now.

No further than – what? - fifteen feet away?

She'd glanced away from him, then back again, whilst his eyes never wandered. How could they? She was all he'd ever dreamed of, secretly and often, and now she was real. *So* real.

Wasn't she?

Suddenly his trance was broken.

At first he felt the gentle push, the nudge against his back, before he felt what could only be teeth, grabbing his sleeve. Then his arm that the teeth – or at least the dog that owned the teeth – was shaking vigorously. Playfully. Thankfully!

'He thinks you've got his ball.'

The beauty – this vision before him – spoke for the first time. *Spoke to him*. The accent was unfamiliar.

'Oh? What...?' was all the sound *he* could manage. His attention was now distracted by the dog, still shaking his arm in playful abandon.

'Can he have it, please...?' She sounded insistent.

'Wha...?'

'The ball. Can he have his ball?'

'...ball?'

'You're *sitting* on it.' Insistence switched to mild irritation as she wondered if this boy was dense.

In the confusion of the tackle, then the fall, then the sight of such a gorgeous creature appearing so unexpectedly before his eyes, he'd been completely oblivious to the fact that another ball – one not associated with his soccer game – was also part of this... this... "what?"'

Then he felt it underneath him, squashed under his right buttock, so far totally unaware to him.

He reached down; his hand retrieved the offending article, at which point the dog scampered off some ten or twenty feet away from them both before turning to face him, trembling in anticipation that the ball would be thrown. The dog barked, as if the say, 'Throw it then, stupid.'

Or maybe she might say it.

It was all too fast for Alan in any case. He was too busy watching her, responding only when she *did* utter those words, 'Throw it then.'

She left off the word 'stupid'.

To the dog's great relief, 'Stupid' did finally throw it. He threw it a long way - so far that it disappeared over the fence – the fence bordering the bank leading up to the railway lines.

'Rupert, stop!' Her irritation changing to panic at the thought of her terrier wandering off onto the lines in search of the lost ball.

'Rupert? What kind of a name is that for a dog?' (Luckily he thought it, but didn't actually say it.*)*

And it was just the break he needed. Leaving the pitch completely now, he trotted off to search for the ball, spotting it a few inches the other side of the fence. He reached through, picking it up as the dog – followed by the girl – approached.

He handed the ball over to the outstretched hand of the girl. On her wrist was a bracelet – and a charm.

'Pisces,' he uttered, his mouth engaging before he

had time to think about what he might say.

'What...?;

'Pisces,' he repeated. 'Your birthday. In March. Probably – about the same time as mine.'

'August, actually. It was my grandmother's'

'Wha...?' Now he was confused.

'My birthday. It's August. The charm – it was my grandmother's. *Her* birthday was in March.' The look on her face was one that said *Why am I bothering to tell him all this?*

But for some reason she had.

Now there was silence.

An embarrassing silence, just the terrier, panting. Tongue out. Peering upwards. Fidgeting.

Staring at the ball.

Waiting.

Chapter Two

Without speaking – neither of them – they began to walk; actually she walked while he followed, but not behind her. He was at her side, ready to go wherever she went. His mind or, at least his rational mind, had switched off. He was in a daze.

It was an unusual picture – she was wearing a smart summer dress with just enough of her slim legs showing to reveal her tan – matched by her bare arms; Alan, on the other hand, whilst sporting a tan to equal hers, looked rather out of place next to her with his soccer shorts and t-shirt.

Their walk was slow and deliberate as if each of them wanted it to last longer than it needed to, taking in the perimeter of the playing field until they'd reached the footpath flanked by a high wall on one side, and allotments on the other. The lane led to Northfield Road then on to the centre of the village.

'I could walk you the whole way home.' Alan's offer was designed not only to extend their first encounter but so that he would know where she lived for the next time.

Assuming there would be a next time.

She hesitated. He tried again.

'That's if you want. It will be dark soon and I just want to make sure you're safe.'

His reassurance and alleged motive convinced her.

'OK, but you can't walk me home looking like that.

In fact no, you'd better not walk me home.'

'I can change,' he protested. 'Just give me two minutes. My clothes are in the Social Centre.'

She agreed. They continued across the park to the gate opening onto the main Leicester Road, with the Social Centre directly opposite. They crossed the road and entered the compound, where she waited outside while he changed quickly into 'street clothes'.

The smile on her face as he emerged from the changing rooms showed her approval. 'A Ben Sherman shirt? Nice. I like them for myself – especially the way they come in at the waist. Perfect with Levis.'

As it turned out she knew what she was talking about. She'd recently started to work at The Irish Linen Company in the Silver Arcade in Leicester. He was impressed – first with her sense of fashion, which was obvious in the way *she* dressed, but also at the prospect of getting his next sports jacket at a discount.

But was his mind moving too fast?

Apparently not.

The remainder of the walk home was filled with conversation about all the other things they seemed to have in common – from pop records to film stars and films to a love of dancing.

Alan lied about that.

To him it was a means to an end – the chance to meet girls – but the opening couldn't be missed.

'Do you go to The Il Rondo, Alan?'

'Well, yes. I have been on the Sunday nights. It's about the only place open. It's just up the road from where you work, isn't it?'

'Fancy taking me next weekend?'

She was asking *him* out? Could he believe it? He had better, because the next question was a clincher.

'Come in and meet my mum... and my sister.'

'Your sis...?'

'I'll explain in a minute.' she added. 'You don't mind, do you?'

What could he say?

So he said nothing.

'Mum, this is Alan,' she announced as soon as they entered the lounge of her parents' house. 'He's offered to escort us to the I Rondo to see The Who.'

'The Who?' It was a question she didn't really understand had two meanings.

'That's right,' said the girl. He'd learnt earlier her name was Anna. 'And here's my sister, Carol.' At the sound of Anna's return Carol had come to see what all the commotion was about. 'Carol, Alan is going to take us to see The Who next week.'

Carol just beamed, but shyly, wondering who was this strange boy Anna had found.

Alan was open-mouthed. Had he been 'had'? He wasn't quite sure but he just went along with it. What did he have to lose? It transpired – from the story Anna's mother told later – that the girls could NOT go on their own to the performance as it was too dangerous for them. Carol was only just over a year older than Anna, and neither had boyfriends – or any other friends or family – locally, after their move into the area. Then along came Alan.

Perfect.

But it became more than that. Alan and Anna did become 'an item' soon after – it was called 'going steady at the time – but it had its ups and downs.

As most relationships do.

If there were any 'downs' to do with sporting two attractive sisters on your arm to a 'Who' performance then he was yet to hear about it. Meanwhile he just bathed in the almost tangible glow of envy from other young blokes - including those from the village or from his soccer team who recognised him.

One of them was Carl, out with a couple of team mates. He quickly decided it would be more fun to tag along with Alan and the girls, a move that would have repercussions further down the line.

Alan accepted Carl's 'attachment' to them as inevitable and without complaint, even though he knew what he was like. Putting up with Carl didn't mean that he was less than happy about it. Carl was renowned for being just a little bit of a 'chancer' when it came to pretty girls. That included those 'attached' to *other* blokes - mates included. Now his presence changed the whole tone of the evening as far as Alan was concerned.

There was suddenly a tension in the air.

The Who's appearance was not a seated affair but more of a dance, with the band commanding the small stage and playing two sets of about fifty minutes each. The opening band were a local group called The Farinas, featuring American-style blues and much more grass-roots than The Who.

They brought along their own followers.

From the outset, as soon as Alan sensed Carl moving in on them he made it pretty clear - to Carl, at least - that Anna was with him. That was assuming there was to be some ongoing 'ownership' or partnership further down the line.

Alan's closeness met with no resistance from Anna, but she sensed the reasons why. As soon as Alan was out of range, Carl seized his chance.

'Care for a dance?' whispered Carl into Anna's ear whilst Alan was buying drinks. Carl was *that* sneaky. But he hadn't counted on Alan being served quite so promptly. Carl's move was followed by a sharp dig in his back from some unknown assailant behind him.

He should have guessed who.

The 'unknown' party was Alan. The result was that Carl's *over*ture was indeed 'over' before it had begun. A splash of ice cold lager down Carl's neck accompanied the dig, not only cooling his ardour, but leading to him needing the men's room to dry off. Anna just looked shocked.

'Sorry, mate,' lied Alan, just managing to disguise his satisfaction as his well-aimed and deliberate spilling of an otherwise over-priced beverage found its mark. 'Oops. Carl! I didn't see you there. Somebody pushed me. Are you OK?'

Even if he had heard it, Carl's response was to ignore the apology, including Alan's almost transparent insincerity. Rather than cause a scene he made his way through the crowded dance-floor to get cleaned up.

By the time he returned, Alan and Anna were well away. His opportunity missed. So what next? It left Carol at the mercy of his team-mate.

But the point had been made.

'Things might have worked out OK,' said Alan, during a relatively slow dance. 'With Carl taking Carol off our hands it leaves us more time together.'

'Are you saying my sister's a liability?'

'No. Not at all.'

'Just kidding,' she assured him, pressing closer. 'She can be a pain. A bit 'clingy' and sometimes with the wrong person - such as with my date.

'But we'd still better make sure she comes back with us. On the bus.' he said.

'Why?'

Alan had no compunction over providing a frank and honest opinion on Carl, based on past experience.

'I just don't trust him. Not with a girl of mine, and not even with the sister of a girl of mine.'

'That's very noble of you,' she said, adding, 'So, I'm your girl am I?'

'If you want to be...'

'Seems I have no choice what with Carl taken.' She was looking across the floor to check on her sister and Carl, but their faces were already locked in what the Mills and Boon novels she'd been reading called 'a passionate embrace'.

Carl had moved fast.

She decided to follow suit, with Alan, taking him completely off guard and unable to protest - leastways not audibly - even if he wanted to. Their first kiss lasted for the whole of the slow number.

'Why does the lead singer stutter?' Anna wanted to know after they'd come up for air. She was referring to Daltrey in the song 'My Generation'.

'I thought you'd know, being such a big fan...'

'I am, but...'

Alan put her out of her misery. 'It's the pills. The uppers and downers they take. It's supposed to have that affect. Give them a speech impediment.'

'*They* take...?

'The Mods. The Car Boys and The Scooter Boys. They take these Purple Hearts and stuff.'

'And *you* don't?' she wanted to know.

'Don't need it,' he said. He was telling the truth.

'What about you?' He was curious about her, now.

'Never occurred to me.'

Chapter Three

It was a good start and would have been a deal breaker - for either of them - if they *had* admitted to taking anything other than alcohol to get high. But the same couldn't be said for Carl, leading to another reason why he felt the responsibility towards Carol as well as to Anna. It was as if he'd sworn an oath to their mother to be sure nothing 'happened' to them.

Now he *couldn't* be sure.

But for now he tried to dismiss his fears - for that was all they were. Fears. He had no proof that Carl would lead her astray in another way, even though he knew Carl would certainly 'try it on' as they say.

That was about to change. Get serious.

His first suspicions arose when he noticed one or two of the scooter boys disappearing towards the Mens' Room. That wouldn't be worthy of note were it not that they *looked* shifty, shifty as in looking around them to see if they'd been spotted by the doormen. But Carl noticed them.

And Alan noticed Carl - he was following them. He was gone just a few minutes, leaving Carol to concentrate on the group. On her own.

'Hand them over,' Alan hissed as Carl re-emerged from the corridor leading back to the dance floor.

Carl's face registered surprise - not only at finding Alan's face just inches away from his own, but at knowing he'd been rumbled. Caught out. Red-handed.

Or, to be more accurate, Purple-handed.

'What the...?' Carl protested.

'Hand them over.'

'Hand what over?' Carl's feigned innocence didn't work. Alan piled on the pressure.

'You know 'what'. Hand 'em over.' He made a grab for Carl's clenched hand.

In the struggle the evidence - the purple evidence - spilled out from Carl's once-clenched fist. It was a shock, combined with delight, for those around. They scooped up the easily-won prizes.

Carl was livid, clenching the other fist and swinging it wildly but so hastily that it glanced off Alan's ear. It was game on. The two players, Carl and Alan, were going at it full on until two door-men sprang to life, relishing in the opportunity to relieve their boredom, replaced by the prospect of mixing it with them. Or anyone.

Blokes looking on cheered while girls screamed - including Carol, and then Anna, as they saw *their* blokes being unceremoniously marched to the exit. It was a beautifully executed performance by the doormen. To their credit not a punch was landed by them in anger or otherwise. Engaging the skill they'd honed during their day job as marines, they simply *and so smoothly*, wrapped heavily muscled arms around each of the protagonists, virtually carrying Carl and Alan out of harm's way of other dancers -

and of each other.

Scuffed knees and elbows from their meeting the harsh reality of the paving slabs outside matched the damaged pride of each. The doormen returned to their posts inside with, 'And don't come back.'

The girls followed.

'Are you nuts?' screamed Carol, at Alan.

'You'd better ask him.' Alan was pointing at Carl.

'Don't know what he's talking about,' whined Carl.

'*I* do.' Anna was now calm, her understanding of why Alan had confronted Carl soon apparent.

She'd seen the 'evidence'.

'Tell her, Carl,' Alan added. Carl whined again.

'I just wanted us to have a really good time.' By 'us' he meant himself and Carol. He was embarrassed more than angry, made all the worse once Anna had explained things to Carol about the drugs, who then confronted Carl herself.

'Call that a good time? Being out of your head? Unless you were trying to...,' she finished the sentence with a slap, rather than words.

'It wasn't anything like that. Honest.'

But it wasn't working. Carl needed support. 'Tell her, Alan. I'm not like that, am I?' Alan's silence didn't help, but Anna stepped in, helping Carl up from where he still lay, hurt in more than one way.

Alan was surprised at this act of kindness, diplomacy even. He'd got to his feet immediately and now merely looked on, thinking, 'Why is she so concerned about Carl, rather than with me?'

Carol joined her, taking over and with a gesture that said, or suggested, at least, that she believed his story. More than that she was reacting to Anna's 'handling' of Carl. He wasn't yet her boyfriend but he was 'hers' - and not her sister's.

No. He was definitely not her sister's. Yet.

Alan felt awkward then relieved as Anna joined him. She apologised. 'I'm sorry, Alan. But you might have been a bit hard on him, don't you think?'

His open mouth said it all. Carl's concealed grin said more, which he hid from the girls. Was it a Pyrrhic victory after all, for Carl?

But Alan spotted it. 'Bastard,' he whispered under his breath - and for good reason. He knew and, even if Carl *had* fooled the girls, *he* wasn't falling for his story. He knew Carl only too well and had seen it before, even on the soccer pitch. He was sneaky. His favourite ploy being the sly tap of the opposite number's ankles if he thought the opponent was getting past him, bringing the player down and then protesting his innocence if the referee blew for a foul.

And it looked like Carl was getting away with 'foul play' again, and nothing Alan could say was going to change the girls' minds. He simply had to put up with it, but he wasn't going to apologise.

Rather than to go straight home they went for a drink. Together. All four of them. The last thing Alan wanted was for the evening to end badly. If it did, it might be the last he would see of Anna. That was too high a price to pay.

But Alan wasn't going to just roll over.

'Looks like it might be your round, seeing that you landed us in this mess.'

Carl didn't even protest this time, heading for the bar as soon as they entered the Churchill. It was fairly empty and in sharp contrast to an hour before when The Il Rondo opened its doors. They found seats next to the Juke Box which Alan fed with half a dozen numbers to fill the otherwise silent bar.

'To friendship.' Carl raised his glass as he toasted what he hoped would be a new start - at least a new start for Alan and Carl, perhaps for the third time. They had fallen out before, mainly on the football field, but this was the first time it had come to blows.

They all raised their glasses in response, with Alan displaying compliance and resisting any sarcasm that might have been intended by Carl.

'We should do this more often,' said Carol, but the glint in her eye - aimed at him - made Alan feel a mixture of intrigue, at her intentions, combined with an irresistible attraction towards her.

After all, she was Anna's sister and they shared the same...something, that Alan couldn't quite define.

Whatever it was it was working.

Anna sensed it too and took up the initiative.

'I do like this number. Care for that dance, Carl?'

Carl was up like a shot, before Alan could think of something to say to stop them, let alone move. There was only one thing for it. He took up the offer from Carol that, just moments earlier, had been nothing more than a vague promise.

But promise of what?

The Churchill were used to people dancing and had left an area cleared of tables just for that purpose. It was a favourite haunt for Mods of every description, whether or not The Who were in town. Its proximity to the Il Rondo assured The Churchill of that. The Juke Box had all the latest records.

And Mods loved to dance.

Anna's apparent move on Carl was aimed more at her sister, rather than at Carl, or even Alan. Just as Alan and Carl shared this rivalry on and off the soccer pitch - if shared is the right word for it - so the two sisters also had their own competition going. In terms of worldliness and social skills there was little distance between them, neither of which made determining who was the older of the two very easy. They could easily have been twins, albeit not truly identical, even their features made it clear from the outset they were sisters. But Anna was prettier.

At least to Alan she was, which made her move on Carl all the more threatening, leaving him with a lack of security that left him uneasy. As attractive as Carol was - he couldn't deny that she was desirable, too - he couldn't wait for the song, and the dance, to end.

It did end - but it was the first of many - with Alan and Anna and Carol and Carl changing partners for the next hour or so - leaving the pub before dancers from The Il Rondo spilled out and repopulated The Churchill. They had to run to The Newarke terminal to make the last bus home.

It was with a restored state of mind and composure that Alan joined the two of them - just the two girls - on the back seat, with Carl taking a different bus.

They didn't talk for most of the journey.

'Shame about missing most of The Who,' said Alan, finally breaking the silence as they passed The County Arms. 'The County', as it was called, had its usual dance every night. Locals from the village clambered on, scrambling for the last of the free seats. Most were also bound for Blaby.

He was sat between the two of them, but holding Anna's hand. 'Thank you for taking us, Alan,' said Anna, giving him an affectionate kiss on the cheek.

'Yes, thank you, Alan,' said Carol, kissing the other. 'I'm sorry Carl made it unpleasant for a time.'

'Will you be seeing him again?' he asked.

Carol paused. 'I'm not sure. He seems a bit nuts but, in a way, that's what I like about him. What do you think, Anna?'

'Glad to hear it,' said Anna. 'But it's your choice.'

'Don't you forget it,' added Carol.

It didn't sound like a threat. Her tone wasn't nasty, but she was making a point. She was reacting to

Anna taking the first chance she had for dancing with Carl in The Churchill, even over Alan. Granted, she'd retaliated immediately by dragging Alan onto the floor, although it met with little resistance *from him*.

In the weeks and months to come it became a familiar pattern, with Carol usually at the centre of it, controlling the play, playing Carl off against Alan and the bewildered Anna stuck firmly in the centre. Anna wanted Alan but was always being pushed towards Carl while Carol secretly tempted Alan.

At first, Alan was suckered into the charade and the games Carol played, such as setting up a foursome but, when Alan turned up to wherever she'd arranged he'd discover it was just himself and Carol. Nor would they be harmless meet-ups for coffee in town, but 'swimming dates' where she could flaunt herself in front of Alan at some out-of-the-way Lido or even a river in the depths of the Leicestershire countryside.

Secret places.

Places where they wouldn't be seen.

Over time her games became more serious and they *did* drive division between Alan and Anna.

Would they become permanent?

Chapter Four

...but that was five years ago.

Even so, those first days were fresh in his memory as he sat in the back of the limousine on the way to the church. Could he ever forget the first time he and Anna had...?

'... did you even hear what I said?' She was sat next to him behind the driver and looking as beautiful as the day he first saw her.

'I'm sorry...?' He glanced across at her, resplendent in her wedding dress, but there was something wrong.

She sniffed as she raised a tissue to her nose, then to her eyes. But there was no mistaking her tears.

'The bastard!' she blurted out. 'And on our wedding day!' She was referring to her wedding to Carl, Alan's best friend, and something he already knew – or had heard – about Carl. He was cheating on her.

'What is it?' Alan pretended he didn't know.

'And with my own sister! She's always been jealous of me – just because she's older and thinks I get more than her.'

'More of what?' His question was ridiculous, but it was too late now.

'Everything!' It was followed by an explosion of tears from Anna, and a comforting arm from Alan.

He was standing in for her father who'd died

suddenly just a few weeks before the wedding. Now it was Alan giving her away to Carl, his best friend.

After Alan and Anna split up a year ago he'd taken up with Carol shortly afterwards and, oh so conveniently, Carl had begun to date Anna.

But he'd since been uneasy about the whole affair – because that's what it seemed like – given that he knew what Carl was like, plus he still had feelings for Anna. He didn't want her to get hurt.

Now she was clearly hurt, at the worst of times.

'I thought it was funny when Carol didn't turn up to get me ready this morning. After all, she was my maid of honour. She was with him on the night before our wedding!'

'...and that's why Carl had left part way through his stag night,' Alan mused. 'To go where?' One of his team-mates told him during last orders at the bar.

'How did you find out?' asked Alan.

'Tracey told me just as we were getting into the car. You should have seen the smug look on her face. *She* hates me *too!*' Anna's make-up was now streaked beyond repair from so many tears. Alan had to think quickly. The church was just ten minutes away.

Where the idea came from, Alan would never know, but it just happened.

'We could do it,' he said.

'Do what?

'Get married, of course.'

'What – now?'

'Yes. Now,' Alan grasped her free hand so she knew he was serious.

Anna wiped her eyes, repairing her make-up as best she could. 'You still want me, then, after...?'

'After Carl? Of course I do,' he said. 'You could say the same to me about Carol.'

Anna was now fighting back the tears, recovering, as if the news – the declaration Alan had just made – was healing the wounds that were, otherwise, so fresh. She gave a final sniff before leaning forward to kiss him. The driver adjusted his rear view mirror.

Away from the scene.

'Let's do it, then,' she said, recovering her breath. 'We'll show them! Who's going to stop us?'

Alan thought for a while. 'The vicar could. We haven't had the bans read. And then the paperwork...'

'Let me take care of that.' Anna was now glowing as if in triumph, the tragedy of just a few minutes ago now a memory.

'How?'

'You'll see. Wait 'till we get there.' She had a plan. 'Driver? When we get to the church, can you nip round the rear to the vestry and call the vicar out to see me? I'll wait near the car.'

The driver, surprised as he was, still agreed.

'What are you up to?' Alan knew it would be something just little dodgy.

'Forget the red tape, I'm making the vicar an offer he can't refuse.' For the first time since they'd left her house, she allowed herself to smile.

'And that is...?'

Well,' she began, excited now at the prospect of making this the happiest day of her life after all, 'you remember that Tracey I was telling you about?'

'Oh – *that* Tracey.'

'That would be the one. What you don't know, and what the vicar – nor Tracey – don't know that *I* know is... they're having an affair.' Her pure delight was showing in abundance. 'So,' she continued, 'when he comes out I'll tell him what I know that he doesn't realise I know – then he'll be putty in my hands.'

'Putty...? I'm confused.'

'He'll do anything I say,' she concluded, not seeing the necessity of spelling it out to Alan.

'Including granting us a special licence,' chuckled Alan, marvelling at the quick-thinking of his soon-to-be new bride. 'Count me in!'

A few short minutes later out came the driver with the vicar in tow, trying to keep up. He was already flustered, agitated – but that was nothing to how he'd be just moments later.

Anna took him to one side, out of earshot of the driver – and Alan – although *he* could only guess what she was saying.

The vicar's face said it all.

The next moment he was scuttling back to the church more red-faced than ever, whilst the driver held open the car door for Alan to join Anna.

'Come on,' she grinned, ' it's all set.'

Alan hesitated for a moment. 'Hang on, what about Carl? Isn't he in there already? Expecting you?'

'The vicar said 'no'. If I'm any judge – and I'm usually right - the bugger's already on his way to the airport on *our* honeymoon – *with Carol*.'

'But...' Alan was dumbstruck.

'If you ask me I'd reckon Tracey – that bitch Tracey – is driving them. He's got our tickets and must have planned it all along.'

'Leaving you at the alter?' Alan seethed. 'You're right. What a bastard!'

Anna grabbed him by the arm.

'Did Jimmy turn up?'

'Jimmy?' she questioned him.

'The Best Man. He's got the ring.' Alan knew that *he* hadn't because he was supposed to be giving her away, not marrying her.

'Let's hope so,' they chorused, before taking a nervous walk towards the church main entrance.

'The other side.'

'What?'

'The other side,' she hissed through her teeth. 'You're not giving me away – you're *taking* me away. You need to be on the right.'

They swapped places to the amusement – and bewilderment - of the two ushers standing inside to greet them. One started to say something.

'Don't worry about it,' Anna reassured him from

the corner of her mouth. 'It'll all become clear soon.'

The usher stepped back, but wouldn't be the only one seeking an explanation.

As they proceeded up the aisle, the bridesmaids – minus a maid of honour – following obediently behind as if they hadn't noticed the difference. They finally stood before the still red-faced vicar nervously shuffling his order of service. He suspected his guilt to be common knowledge by now to all those around them, even though it was one of Anna's well-kept secrets. Guilt has an amazing knack for blowing a simple misdemeanour out of all proportion for the guilty. Luckily, Jimmy wasn't part of the conspiracy and had turned up – complete with wedding ring and totally innocent of what had been going on.

Alan's first thoughts were, 'At least that's saved me a few quid on a ring!'

He was still smiling as he turned back to Anna.

She was now as radiant as ever, somehow – who knows how – managing to fix her make-up with no sign of a tear or smudged mascara.

She was smiling up at him. Beaming. Triumphant.

What followed next went smoothly enough given the circumstances, right through the ceremony, the reception (already booked and paid for by Carl), not to mention the endless questions. The story behind the real drama, varying with each successive telling, was repeated countless times. All the guests appeared to be satisfied and happy for the couple apart from Carl's family. They'd made a discreet departure once they were privy to the truth – the detail that both Alan and Anna decided not to share to a wider world.

As far as most were concerned, in a fit of 'buyer's remorse' the previous day (by Carl), the solution presented itself (for Alan and Anna) to rekindle the love they first had, and for the flame to be reignited, fuelled by circumstance.

The precise nature of those circumstances was no-one else's business. It was as much as they needed to know; and as much as they were going to know. Faces and reputations had been 'saved' - as far as that were possible, and desirable.

The honeymoon was in the Lake District thanks to a last minute car hire and hotel rooms booked by phone on the day. Ten days alone together.

Ten *glorious* days.

The one thing Carl had not taken with him were keys to the flat that he and Anna had moved into and furnished a month earlier.

Once back from The Lakes Alan and Anna changed the locks.

Just in case.

~ *** THE END *** ~

The Black Hound of Dartmoor

A tale of moorland myth, legend and romance

By J S Morey

First published in Great Britain 2023

Further reading:

The series 'Love should never be this hard':

Book 1: The Sign of the Rose
Book 2: The Black Rose of Blaby
Book 3: Rose: The Missing Years
Book 4: Finding Rose

Wild Hearts Roam Free – Wild Hearts Come Home
Two modern westerns set in Wyoming
Unresolved? - a short story linked to 'Wild Hearts Roam Free'

Those Italian Girls – set in the hills of Tuscany

Read My Shorts – short stories and poems with a message

Wood-Spirit - an anthology of poems about trees

For more by this author

visit www.newnovel.co.uk

Chapter One

The farm was asleep in an afternoon sun.

The sudden sound - a panel in the barn door cracking in the dry heat - disturbed the border collie from her slumbers. She lay in the centre of the yard sprawled on her back, but she soon closed her eyes again, breathing heavily as sleep overtook her. Seconds later she was yelping and kicking furiously, eyes still closed - racing across some imaginary field, acting out a familiar dream chasing rabbits. She ceased as they darted to safety into bolt-holes.

Some things never change.

Calm descended again, peace returning to the Devon longhouse built into the hillside for protection against foul weather. But there was no protection from the hot sun. A light summer breeze swept down from the hillside and through the willow tresses creating a whooshing sound, before coming to rest as quickly as they'd disturbed the silence.

The coolness of the air provided welcome relief from the hot rays baking the moor that afternoon.

'Tis like a cauldron on days like this,' yawned the farmer. He, too, had been disturbed by the barn door, which now decided to open and close repeatedly at the bidding of the fractious breeze, still complaining. Daniel surveyed the pot of cider by his chair. It was nearly empty so he drained it in a swallow.

Now *he* complained. 'Ugh! Warm.'

'Bit early for that, anyway, Dan me boy,' said Bessie, his young wife. She called him 'boy' but it was she who was his junior by some thirty years - marrying as she had for security at first but, nevertheless, not without a touch of love, later.

His first wife was taken early. Scarlet fever.

Meanwhile Bessie continued knitting, her needles clicking eagerly as they seemed to sense her own impatience to complete the waistcoat she'd chosen.

Daniel pondered thoughtfully on her last remark in the hope of finding some justification. Or excuse.

He found one.

'Or late,' he eventually replied, 'if you call it my lunchtime sup.'

Her 'humph' showed a resignation at his remark.

'Best I go check the sheep in that far grazing afore suppertime,' he said, his old bones straining to bear his not inconsiderable bulk as he rose from his chair.

Bessie stayed put, determined to finish at least two pockets before she had to prepare supper. They'd both taken rare advantage in the fine afternoon to sit out - together - in the garden overlooking the yard. Daniel had risen early that morning, as usual, keen to lift a few bales while the weather held. But he was still careful to wait until the sun had been up a few hours. It was essential for them to be dry before storing for the winter. The last thing he wanted was to be in too much of a hurry to stack them inside, too green and still damp from the heavy morning dew, only to be awakened in the middle of the night weeks later with the barn alight.

He didn't have to know about spontaneous combustion from the little schooling to which he'd been privy, to understand the dangers of stacking hay before its moisture content was low.

He made his way to the end of the Devon Longhouse. It was where his collie's lay, also taking a nap. A century or two previously it might have been the winter quarters for a milker and her calf, but now it was home to his three sheepdogs.

'Come on, George, Millie, stir yourselves,' he called out, soon joined by the third, Jenny, who'd been the one asleep in the yard. She instinctively responded to her master's voice.

They took their time as the sun continued to beat down on them; flies were irritating the mare as she shook her head and flicked her ears for some respite.

It was a fair distance to the far meadow on foot and across the fields, so he'd elected to take the pony and trap rather than walk. Once a rarity to take the easier option, it was now a habit even on the best of days. It meant taking a different route, along narrow lanes banked high either side by earth, stone and hawthorn. They provided welcome shade for the most part. The pony and trap often saved Daniel's legs if any of the sheep needed carrying back to the farm for any treatment. He had the back of the trap always ready to carry them home, carrying an injured or sick lamb across his shoulders no longer physically possible.

Oh, and there was a third benefit afforded by the small rig. If he made decent time completing the task, *and* if there was nothing serious arising during his stock inspection, he might even manage a jar or two of cider at The Saracen's Head before going home. He knew he was on safe ground thanks to the kindness and understanding of his beloved Bessie.

It had been the first quality he noticed on first meeting her at the village dance, the evening after the Widecombe Fair. Granted, he was just a little worse for wear by ten o'clock - he'd arrived late after a few jars at the pub beforehand - but, as he would often say many a time afterwards (and a saying usually reserved for buying stock at market) he could spot a good 'un when he saw one.

It was therefore not surprising she took her time cooking supper, as usual, anticipating a few jars of cider might still be on his 'to-do' list.

By the time Daniel reached the far grazing, cloud cover had turned a balmy day into one where chill air from the north east made him turn up his collar. Fearing it might even threaten rain, he looked for tell-tale signs. His eyes swept the crest of the nearby tors for tentacles of mist creeping towards him. The horizon was clear - for the time being.

'Woah,' he called soothingly to the mare. It was

the signal for all three dogs to leap off the trap, anticipating its coming to a halt. They made for the gap at the base of the dry-stone wall next to the stile, put there for badgers as well as working dogs. They shot through, running in circles as they chased each other excitedly, not waiting for their master.

'Steady, you lot,' cursed Daniel, fearful the sheep might get too scatty and bolt. It only took one to lead the rest. It wouldn't be the first time they'd clambered over the stone wall bordering the pound, escaping into the open moor. That would be most inconvenient and unnecessary, delaying his trip to the The Saracen's where, in *his* eyes, a well-earned couple of pints had his name on them.

He started out on his inspection at a measured pace. The boundary wall was about 300 paces in circumference, usually taking him twenty minutes or so allowing for 'stoppages' if a section of wall needed a quick repair. The little Dartmoor ponies were usually to blame for the damage. They had a habit of using the tops of the walls on which to scratch themselves which, sometimes, toppled loose stones, lowering the wall sufficient for Daniel's White Face sheep to escape. This time he was in luck. Thanks to the absence of the other fear - bluebottles - none of the flock seemed to be suffering from maggots.

Once Daniel had joined them the three border collies quickly settled down, remaining close and ever vigilant to commands their master might bestow upon them. They followed quietly now at a respectful distance until they were back at their starting place. Without bidding, they scrambled back onto the trap. They were ready for the off.

The mare struck a brisk pace, motivated perhaps by her own thirst. After ten minutes, mindful that The Saracens was their next destination, the collies were soon wagging their tales and barking in turn, in expectation of a morsel of meat that might come their way. There was usually at least someone in the bar generous enough to share the last of their stew.

The landlord's boy had heard the commotion and came out to greet them, taking the reins of Daniel's pony and leading her to a trough of cool spring water. Daniel made his way into the darkness of the public bar, a line of collies behind him. He tossed his coppers over the bar counter in payment just as the jar of scrumpy slid across the smooth wooden counter top to where he stood.

'Looks like 'e's ready for 'e,' announced the landlord. After years of practice judging the distance from himself to a customer's outstretched hand, the landlord made sure each welcome jar arrived at its destination without a drop spilt. Daniel drained half the jar in energetic gulps before replying, exhaling, then bringing up wind trapped inside his gullet.

'Been a long day,' said Daniel, justifying his thirst.

By now, his eyes had adjusted to the gloom so he could make out the familiar face of each neighbour. He raised his jar in acknowledgement to them in turn then drained it completely, setting it firmly down on the bar for a refill.

He acknowledged each fellow drinker, in turn.

'Jim...Jonno...Mark...,' he called, tossing another couple of coppers on the counter in payment.

But someone was missing.

'Where's Peter? Bit late ain't 'e?'

He spoke too soon. Heads turned immediately door-wards as the latch clattered sharply. Peter burst in our of breath, panting.

'Thought I'd find you 'ere, Dan,' he gasped. 'You better get 'ome real quick.' Daniel put down his jar, its contents as yet untouched. He waited for Peter to catch his breath, impatient for him to explain.

'What's goin' on?'

'They're at your place. I saw 'em go in. I rushed straight over 'ere. You need to get back.'

'*Who* went in...?'

'King Billy's men. Four of 'em. Armed, they was. Two on 'oss-back, another two with th'oss pulling a meat wagon.

'They come to arrest 'e, s'far as I could tell.'

Daniel headed for the door then turned back, grabbing his full jar of cider, downing it in one go. Wiping his sleeve across his wet chin, he hurried outside. His dogs followed, beating him to the rig as he rushed to untie his pony and trap. He leapt onto the bench seat, catching hold of the reins. The weight of Daniel in itself, plus the three dogs, was enough to stir the mare into action. Used to such emergencies from time to time, she responded instantly to Daniel's bidding, starting at a trot then gathering pace as they joined the highway, heading for home.

'Come on, old gel,' urged Daniel, to which the dogs echoed in unison, barking their encouragement at the mare. But he knew she was doing her best and, as always, spared the reins or whip. Was it his imagination or did the mare really pick up speed at the behest of the dogs? The journey from The Saracens usually took twenty minutes at normal pace, allowing for Daniel to stop on the way to wet the wheel of the trap. He had no time for that diversion now. He made it home in ten. The mare arrived lathered up as they entered the farmyard. He dropped the reins. Despite his sixty years he jumped from the trap, in haste to find Bessie. She met him half way, emerging tearfully from the kitchen.

He gathered her up in his strong arms.

Chapter Two

'They didn't catch you, then?' Bessie was drying her eyes with her apron. 'I told 'em you weren't 'ere and sent them up over to Bellever, saying you'd gone to borrow some feed from Jedediah Hannaford.'

'Course they didn't catch us,' said Daniel. 'We'm 'ere ain't us?' He regretted his sharp tone as soon as the words left him.

'Sorry, Bess darlin'. Did they 'urt 'e?'

'No. They were a bit shittern faced when I told 'em you were out. Disappointed they was. Came all the way from Tavistock they 'ad, with an arrest warrant. But once they'd cooled down they were quite kind as if they didn't enjoy what they'd been asked to do. They frightened me. They could see I was upset.'

'What's this warrant all about?'

'Said you'd killed a man. They got witnesses. Came to take you back in that there meat wagon.'

'How come they didn't wait 'ere for me?'

'Wanted to get back to Tavy afore dark. 'fraid of the 'airy 'and, I suppose.'

'You tellum that old tale?'

'Might 'ave slipped out.' Bessie managed a guilty smile, she was a bit sheepish, but calmer. 'For once it's just as well you stopped off at The Sarry.'

Cider has a certain smell about it, especially prominent on a person hot after exertion or over-excitement. He didn't bother asking her how she knew about the Saracens. She was looking for more than a confession from him on something she knew he would have done anyway. It wouldn't be the first time he stopped off after work. But kill a man?

'So *did* you?' she asked.

'Did I *what*?'

'*Kill*...whoever it was. You *were* there yesterday, on market day. And you *did* act a bit strange when you got back. Finally.'

'So I was. There, I mean. But I only tapped 'im. Knocked 'im out. Slightly.'

'Knocked 'im out? Slightly?' she asked, not convinced. 'How 'ard?'

'Just a little. Like I said, 'twas just a tap.'

'For no good reason, I suppose?' said Bessie.

'He was cheatin'.' It was no good. The words were out. He'd given *himself* away. Daniel turned away to hide *his* guilt. He'd promised he wouldn't get drawn into a game or two at market.

But the truth was out.

'Gambling? Again?' Bessie was now about to explode.

'But I was *winnin'*.'

'How much?'

'I spent it,' he confessed.

'On what? Don't see no extra vittles.'

'On this.'

His surprise for her was still in his coat, the same

coat he wore to market. It was also the same coat he wore every day, except Sundays.

Today was Saturday.

He knew she loved jewellery. He reached into the depths of his inside pocket, hoping it was still there from yesterday. It was safe; *he* was safe.

By the look on her face it worked as planned.

'Ah... it's...beautiful,' she said, her tone now softened, as had her temper, overcome by the brilliance of the cameo brooch he placed so lovingly into her hand.

But she quickly regained her wits, spotting his motive and remembering the harsh words they'd just exchanged, and why.

'Worth dying for, maybe; but not worth killing for...' She made it know he wasn't out of the woods.

'I didn't kill him. He wasn't dead,' he protested.

'Just a tap, you say.'

'That's right. Just a little tap. After he cheated.'

'Cheated? At...?'

'Devil Among the Tailors,' said Daniel, as if that revelation made everything alright.

'How can anyone cheat at that?'

'He knocked 'em over with his 'and, 'and I saw 'im do it. So did the others. I got witnesses too!'

'So you 'tapped' him?'

'Slightly,' repeated Daniel, making a harmless sweeping of his hand in thin air to stress how gently he'd 'tapped' him.

'But you still won?'

'Yes.'

So where's the rest of the money?' Brooch or now brooch, she wasn't letting him off lightly.

'Ah...,' Daniel said, in a way that told Bessie there was another confession due. 'That's the other thing.'

'You mean there's *more*?' Her patience was being tested.

'Yes. He didn't pay up.'

'But the cameo...' She seemed puzzled.

'Not all of it,' he explained. 'On the last throw, when he lost, he paid me in silver coin then got up to go. But when I went to pick it up... it vanished. The coins turned into leaves and just blew away as soon as he opened the tavern door.'

Daniel paused, studying her face to see if she had more questions to ask. But she hadn't. So he continued.

'That's when I went after him... *and tapped him.*'

'With your hand?'

'Yes,' he confirmed, 'although here's the other thing. My hand was holding a jar of cider.'

Bessie exploded again. 'You hit him with...?'

'It was empty. I promise. The jar was empty. You don't think I'm stupid enough to waste a full jar of cider, do 'e?'

His air of righteousness was not convincing.

'You really *do* want me to answer that?' she asked, after which they both fell silent. It was a lot of information to take in, at least for Bessie.

And a lot to unburden...for Daniel.

Then something dawned on her, something very profound; so much so she shuddered at the thought running through her head.

She spoke. But in a whisper.

'You don't think...?' she began.

'Nah.' He knew what she was going to say.

'Why not?' she continued.

'But that was nearly two hundred years ago.'

'Same name,' she said confidently. 'The Tavistock Inn, Poundsgate, right after a bolt of lightning struck Widecombe Church...'

'...and Tavistock where I struck...,' he concluded.

'Struck the Devil himself,' she said with a sense of finality.

'I'd better confess,' he said after a while.

'What?'

'Why not? Who's going to convict someone for killing The Dark One?'

She had to admit he had a point...

It was noon the following day before Daniel and Bessie arrived at the magistrate's office in Tavistock. It was only after a series of debates that lasted all evening and which, even though at times they reached what could be best described as 'argument level', resulted in Daniel, for once, the victor.

After that it was a sleepless night for two reasons.

First, there was the dilemma of proving to the magistrate it was, indeed, The Dark One who Daniel had 'tapped', apparently resulting in his death. The second question was whether the authorities would, in fact, accept that it was lawful to kill the Devil himself. They had no visible proof of his identity - assuming they believed Daniel's defence - but they still decided to send soldiers with a warrant for his arrest the day. It was those questions that occupied most of their thoughts as they set out for Tavistock.

'I do hope they got back alright.' Bessie chuckled to herself as the pony and trap trotted gamely past The Saracen's Head, casting a nervous eye across to Wiseman's Wood. She was especially aware of the myths and legends surrounding the mysterious standing stones at Merrivale and the Prehistoric Settlement, mindful of how she'd sown the seeds of the Hairy Hand, planting fearful thoughts in the King's men the previous day.

Was she feeling guilty?

Not really. They were soldiers, after all.

But then her own fears were stirred - Daniel's too - as the mare flinched at something moving behind a large patch of gorse by the roadside.

'What's *that*?' she asked. Daniel was dismissive.

'Better ask the mare. Didn't see nothin'.'

'There it goes again, looks like...' Bessie had seen something moving. Now Daniel had, too.

'...a black dog,' he added.

'Big 'un, too,' she agreed. 'You don't think it's...'

'The Black Hound? Nah,' Daniel said. 'He's off down Dean Combe way, if he exists at all, that is.'

Whatever it was, the unexplained rustling and fleeting sighting was enough to spook them, as well as the mare. Plus, it was no coincidence the haunting by a large black dog, said to be the ghost of Weaver Knowles, was alleged to be a regular occurrence at a pool near Dean Prior, albeit quite a distance away, towards Plymouth.

It was uncanny they'd both had the same thought.

Whatever it was - and it could have been no more than a Galloway foraging in the thicket - it was enough for the mare to gather pace, quick to put Merrivale behind them. Daniel and Bessie gave the pony her head and, before too long, the hour or so journey came to an end ahead of time.

They headed straight for the magistrate's office.

Luckily the coroner was in attendance even though it was a Saturday and, surprisingly he was in a receptive and jovial mood. It was almost with some relief that he welcomed them into his study, showing no surprise to find them seated in front of him. That said, it may have been a surprise that Daniel wasn't shackled and delivered at the King's pleasure.

Even though the official wasn't able to receive him within the jurisdiction or formal setting of a public hearing, he still listened intently to Daniel's side of events. Much to Daniel and Bessie's annoyance he continued to react with some levity verging on amusement. This wasn't helped by the fact he allowed Daniel to finish *the whole story* in finest detail before he, the coroner, admitted the reason for his lack of formality and rather bemused interest.

Bessie certainly *didn't* take kindly to his attitude and came straight to the point.

'So what's so funny?'

The coroner raised a hand to his mouth to stifle his laughter as he replied. 'All this has been enlightening, Mr Sercombe, but for one important factor.'

'And that is...?' asked Bessie, on behalf of Daniel.

'As I was about to say, Madam, in order for a... shall we say, death... to have occurred, there has to be a body. A dead body.'

That strange statement drew nothing more than blank looks from Bessie and Daniel, until he couldn't stand it any more. Should he keep quiet or, if he did say any more, would it just make things worse for him? Deepen his guilt?

He decided to risk it.

'But you have it. The body. You took him. I *saw* you carry him off on a stretcher from where I was, across the road from The Queens Head, just before I slipped away to head home. I thought he'd just been knocked out, unconscious but still alive.

'Either way, you've definitely got him.'

The coroner adopted a more official tone.

'I'm afraid... or should I say *I'm happy* to say, that's no longer the case and I have no evidence to suggest otherwise. The person, whoever or whatever you 'tapped', as you so eloquently describe it, has disappeared. Escaped. Vanished. The vault into which he'd been deposited overnight was secure, untouched but, even so, was found empty the next morning.

'All they found was a pile of dry leaves.'

Those last words from the coroner chilled them to the bone. The coroner remained unphased, continuing in his dismissal, ushering them to the door.

'Without a body there can be no death, whatever happened. No death - no charge to answer.'

'So...?'

'So you're free to go.'

Daniel and Bessie were dumbstruck.

'Free?'

'Totally,' the coroner confirmed, 'and, if you will forgive the pun, *you can take your leaves.*'

He closed the door behind them.

Chapter Three

A month passed since the incident in Tavistock, but questions still remained unanswered. Whatever the truth behind it, whether Daniel *had* encountered The Dark One in that wager in the pub on market day - or not - the mysterious ending still haunted him. But on reflection, in his mind's eye it *hadn't* ended.

Was the person he'd simply 'tapped' (as far as he was concerned, and ignoring the fact that he was holding his drinking vessel at the time) was *that* person real or imagined? If so, he wasn't the only one in the pub with a vivid imagination. They'd all seen 'the person'. As the King's men stated when they came to serve the warrant, 'there were witnesses'.

But *was* he dead, or simply unconscious? And, if he really *was* the spectre Bessie insisted he must have been, was he simply playing a trick on everyone in general and on Daniel in particular, true to his character? *Pretending* to be dead but actually alive and only *feigning* death just to get Daniel in trouble?

He'd had a month to turn it over and over in his head. With extended hindsight the more he thought, the more it made sense. By whatever means this spectre of a figure had managed to achieve it, by trickery or otherwise, he'd been able to 'raise himself from the dead'. He'd released himself from the mortuary vaults, escaping into the night. There was another clue that seemed to support this theory.

His horse.

The black stallion upon which he, allegedly, had arrived earlier at Tavistock market, and which he'd left stabled at the Queen's Head to be fed and watered, was gone the next morning.

Now, a horse of that pedigree and value would have been a prime target for thieves. That was one possibility. He was stolen. However, the stable lad always slept overnight above the stalls and had neither heard, nor seen, anything. That said - and this is pure speculation - it wouldn't have been beyond the wit of someone with the kind of powers possessed by The Dark One, to spirit the own horse away, literally, whilst the stable boy slept. The next morning the stall was empty even though neither a latch nor a lock had been disturbed or broken. There was no sign at all of entry nor exit by anyone, nor any*thing*. No evidence of such, except for a pile of leaves scattered on the otherwise clean bedding. *Dead* leaves.

Should Daniel be worried?

As things turned out he was off the hook as it were, and free of any criminal charges, whether for simple assault or even murder. But it wouldn't be from the authorities that he should fear reprisals - not from The Crown, in any case. Not any more.

A full month had passed. No harm had beset either himself or Bessie. Nor did he, nor Bessie, have any close family against whom revenge could be metered. He'd had a son but, as far as he knew, he was dead.

Perished, so the story was told, lost at sea fighting Napoleon in one of the many naval battles.

It was something Daniel never spoke about, but he thought about his loss now.

It had been another source of disquiet and unease Daniel felt increasingly over time, linked in part to his being some thirty years older than his beloved Bessie. When it was time for Daniel to finally depart this earth and with Bessie left to fend on her own - a probability rather than a mere possibility - he had no heir to take over the tenancy. Bessie would be tossed out onto the street with no male family member to run the farm. It was a condition of the tenancy.

But he began to notice other things, notably a feeling of being watched. His dogs felt it too. They often growled at nothing in particular *as far as he could see*, but sensed a presence. Sometimes it might be a rustling behind a scattering of rocks on open moor or behind a hedgerow on the road out to The Saracens. It made his skin crawl, especially when the menace seemed so intense that George, Millie and Jenny would all stand barking at thin air, refusing to move from the spot when Daniel commanded.

They appeared to be protecting him.

But from what?

The story of a black dog haunting the pool at Deancombe was still fresh in the minds of many locals in the area - including Daniel and Bessie. She used the same knitting yarn as the recently deceased

Weaver Holmes, travelling to buy it from the same cottagers near Buckfastleigh who used to supply the much maligned weaver. She'd dismissed the stories of his allegedly returning from the grave to haunt the aptly renamed Hound Pool - assuming it was just a story created and circulated by owners of the large country estates to deter poachers. Now she wasn't so sure, and she instilled that fear into Daniel.

And then there was similarity with the tale of the visit of The Dark One to collect his debt from local gambler Jan Reynolds, who'd fallen asleep in Widecombe church during the service. On his way to the church, The Dark One had stopped by at The Tavistock Inn, Poundsgate, to ask directions. He took refreshment, rode away but, as the landlord went to pick up the coins left in payment for his ale, they turned into dry leaves and blew away.

Those similarities were too close for comfort.

Weeks passed without event until Daniel's next visit to Tavistock market. This time he was allowed to go on one condition, one to which he'd promised Bessie and was foremost in his mind - that he should abstain from gambling *of any kind.*

He kept his word.

He'd also kept reasonably sober and, by mid-day had turned a profit, having sold all his produce. That included the three brace of partridge he bagged a day or two before on Corndon. He'd had his eye on the birds a few weeks beforehand and had bided his time before bagging them, leaving it to the last minute before adding them to his quota, so they would be fresh to market. He sold them all.

There was just one drawback.

His prospective buyer, although well-known to Daniel for being trustworthy, insisted that Daniel deliver the birds to his farm, where his wife would see that he was paid. Again, gambling had played its part, the sport having stripped the buyer - not Daniel - of immediate funds with which to settle his account. But Daniel wasn't stupid. He wasn't going to part with his birds without payment. The drawback was that the buyer lived in Yelverton.

It was a little out of the way, but do-able.

It was barely past noon, so Daniel agreed to the arrangement and struck for home early, allowing time for a diversion. The real drawback only came shortly after Daniel had left Yelverton. He was free of the produce he'd taken to market and full of funds, and eager to prove to Bessie how well he'd done.

What could possibly ruin such a successful day?

He was soon to find out.

The mare had also fared well that day, taking the journey to market in her stride. On the way home, although hesitating and seeming to challenge Daniel at being driven southwards to Yelverton, rather than immediately east via Princetown, they were making good progress.

That's when Daniel's eagerness got the better of him.

A short-cut via Foxtor Mires could trim a mile or two off the journey. He'd a found a track wide enough to take a pony and trap before, not through the midst of the boggy expanse, but along the fringes. It worked. As long as they didn't stray.

At least today it was clear, in full daylight.

All seemed to be going well until the once sunny day turned chilly and wet and, worst of all, misty. Within ten minutes Daniel was engulfed in a blanket of cloud, not able to see more than a few yards ahead of himself or the mare, even though there were still hours of daylight left. On they drove but slowly now, any prospect of saving time lost. Their main purpose was to simply get home safe.

It's said that Dartmoor ponies are able to pick their way through the mires, avoiding sinking into the quakers - deep watery bogs covered with moss and resembling firm ground to the unwary. Ponies trace well-trodden paths to get from one area of solid ground to the other. Daniel willing to believe it to be true, trusting the mare to choose the right route, east, even if they did stray with no telling where they might come out. It wasn't until they arrived at a fork in the now almost unrecognisable track that the mare hesitated. Should she fork left? or right?

Her mind was about to be made up for her.

She heard, then saw, something through the mist.

She blew heavily, steam billowing from her nostrils as an unfamiliar figure appeared before them. Daniel's heart was pounding in his chest. The shape drew closer and its identity became clearer. Just a little.

It wasn't a *human* shape.

From its size he first took it to be a Dartmoor foal, but he wasn't sure - a foal on its own? With no mare? Then its identity became certain. It was a large dog; a large *black* dog. But was everything really as it appeared to be? His thoughts turned immediately to Weaver Knowles and the hound into which, so the story went, he'd turned when cursed by the local parson. Should he be afraid?

Should he fear for his life?

Strange as it may seem, he didn't think so.

He was surprised at himself as well as at the mare, when a sudden calm came over both of them. Instead of threatening or even attacking them, the black hound turned away from them slowly, taking the left fork in the path. It even seemed to beckon. The mare reacted first, unchallenged and unaided by Daniel as she followed the black shape closely, mists swirling about them. The hound continued silently and confidently ahead of them, only occasionally looking round to make sure they still followed.

It was so quiet; so deathly quiet, even the skylarks were silent.

The only sound was of occasional hooves on loose

stone, and the creaking of the trap as the uneven path strained the loose joints of the tailgate. There were no birds singing, no breeze to disturb gorse, rowan or what few stunted trees there were; only the trickle of small streams and rivulets draining into the mires.

A group of magpies lay quietly in the wet grassland as if in wait. Some might call them 'a charm of magpies', or others 'a murder of magpies', perhaps depending on their intent. They allowed the black hound to pass before rising suddenly, deliberately startling the mare as the trap drew up alongside. It took her off guard causing her to rear up. Her sudden, defensive movement unbalanced the trap and Daniel, one wheel now suspended in the air. It tipped sideways, sufficiently to topple Daniel backwards, over into the mire below.

As he was falling the birds swooped over him in celebration at seeing an unfortunate becoming yet another victim of Foxtor Mires. Was it Daniel's imagination or did he hear voices over him chanting the familiar nursery rhyme he'd learnt as a small boy at school, about the the fortune awaiting us on the sight of magpies:

One for sorrow, Two for joy,
Three for a girl, Four for a boy,
Five for silver, Six for gold,
Seven for a secret never to be told.
Eight for a wish, Nine for a kiss,

Ten for surprise no wiseman should miss,
Eleven for health, Twelve for wealth,
Thirteen beware it's the devil himself...
How many birds were there?

He landed well enough. It was soft; too soft. The weight of his coat and the waters of the bog filled his boots dragging him down. He was stuck. All he could do was cry for help for someone to save him.

But who? The birds continued to dive overhead.

The hound responded first. The mare was purely intent on saving herself by not allowing the trap to drag her in with him. She forced herself up and managed to take a few short steps forward until the weight of the trap was no longer pulling on her down.

But what of Daniel?

The more he thrashed about the more he seemed to sink. Throwing caution to the wind he tentatively allowed his feet to reach down, hoping to find solid ground, but to no avail. He just sank lower. But who was that 'someone' coming to his rescue?

Certainly not someone he expected.

It was the black hound.

He came trotting back to the edge of the quaker into which Daniel had been thrown. But what could a hound do? How could he drag the weight of a fully grown man out of the sticky mass of the bog without getting into trouble himself? Then the inexplicable happened. The black hound changed shape.

Into a man.

The black fur of what once covered an Irish Wolfhound gradually changed into human clothing: a hat, a black cape, breeches and black boots, clothing of the kind worn by someone of some wealth and social standing. It was clearly no ordinary man and not a peasant farmer or labourer. As the mist cleared slightly Daniel recognised him. But he hardly believed his eyes. From the drawings and sketches he'd seen in the local gazette when they covered stories of the haunting of Deancombe Pool he was now certain, as impossible as it might seem. It was none other than Knowles - Weaver Knowles.

But he was dead, wasn't he?

'Reach out with the end of your cane,' the weaver called. 'I'll pull you in if I can only find the strength.'

Daniel reached out, as did Knowles, catching the end of the cane and pulling. But it was no good. The sludge and slime of the boggy mire was so slippery, Knowles couldn't keep a firm grip. He tried again, and again but, after each attempt, Daniel sank slowly deeper and deeper. Panic set in.

The magpies continued their morbid aerial dance.

Knowles was now so close to Daniel that, even as the mist thickened again and swirled around them, he could still make out his distinctive features. He could see tears streaming down Knowle's face as panic overtook him, too. He spoke once more, his voice trembling as he sensed Daniel slipping away.

'I fear I am losing you, sir. I am so sorry. It grieves me to fail you in death, just as I failed so many others in life. Since departing this earth I have made it my pledge to help my fellow man, making up for all the wickedness and greed I bestowed on poor cottagers, friends and neighbours when I lived.

'It is now my mission to help the weary or lost traveller, to save crops from ruin by storm, to rescue young lambs fallen into stream or river, and to help the poor farmer bring home the harvest if they lack family or funds to pay itinerant workers for the task.

'If I cannot save you now, sir, which seems unlikely, is there anything I can do to compensate or to comfort those you leave behind? A wife, perhaps? Son, or daughter?'

'Bessie,' shouted the frantic Daniel as the waters of the mire finally closed around him. 'Give her my love, make sure she never goes hungry or is without shelter and, if the Good Lord wills it, find a way for her to keep the farm. Don't let them take it away.

'Bessieeeee....!'

So he perished, a miserable fate but with a final wish, the name of his beloved on his lips as he sank.

He was gone, disappeared, swallowed up in the murky depths of Foxtor Mires.

The thirteen magpies were nowhere to be seen.

Chapter Four

As wicked, mercenary or unpopular as Knowles might have been in life, in death his spirit still lived with the sole (or should that be *soul*?) purpose of providing succour and spreading goodness. For the sake of convenience and so that he remained largely unrecognised and undetected he'd assumed the shape and existence of a black hound.

Most of the time. It also meant that in the main, folk would leave him alone - out of fear.

Remorse at not being able to save the drowning man swept over him as he knelt in prayer over the spot where Daniel had met his cruel fate. Eventually he rose, going over to where the mare still stood, oblivious to the tragedy that had befallen her master. As natural as such an unnatural act could ever be, he changed back into the black hound, but out of sight of the mare for fear of frightening her.

He made his way to the front of the pony and trap, ahead of where the mare stood, taking the reins in his teeth. He led them safely away from the perils of Foxtor Mires. It made sense to report the matter and it was the least he could do, rather than leave Daniel's disappearance undetected and unexplained to loved ones. The mare was unphased by the presence of the hound and, by assuming the guise of an animal, Knowles could reply on survival instincts and senses most suited to negotiating the wilds and dangers of the remote moorland.

Less than an hour later the farm came into view. By that time the mist had risen, allowing them clear vision, sun and warmth, as they completed the rest of the journey in safety. They did so but without Daniel and without his body, which was never found.

Years later Daniel still hadn't resurfaced.

As for Weaver Knowles, he entered the farm gates *as Knowles* but not looking forward to delivering his account of Daniel's sad demise. In life, his ability to persuade, negotiate, and to spin a plausible tale had been part of his success. He applied those skills when explaining Daniel's fate to the distraught Bessie.

As awful as that task was, for both Knowles and for Bessie, she appeared to accept his death with relative calm after the initial shock. A few glasses of port and brandy also helped. She even offered Knowles supper followed by a soft mattress for the night in the guest room. It had been the room of Daniel's boy, William, before he'd left home.

It was midnight when they retired, separately.

Dawn broke with Bessie rising early as usual, to the crowing of the Rhode Island Red cockerel. Her first task was to feed George, Millie and Jenny. After that she braved the chilly morning air, crossing the yard with the collies in train, to fetch a fresh warm pale of milk from her favourite Devon Red milker. Ten minutes later she had eggs, bacon and tomatoes -

plus foraged fungi - frying away on the stove with a kettle boiling for a pot of tea.

She wasn't exactly quiet whilst preparing breakfast and therefore surprised not to hear the boards in the guest room creaking overhead. She assumed the noise and smell of bacon would stir Knowles into going about his ablutions. She called up the stairs.

No answer. She waited - and called again.

In the absence of a sound *of any kind* she climbed the stairs hesitantly, calling as she ascended, finally arriving at the closed door to the guest room.

She knocked gently.

No answer. She knocked again, slipping open the latch as she did so to enter the room. To no-one. The bed was undisturbed, the room empty.

Knowles had gone.

She cast her eyes around the room for any signs that he'd actually been there, but there was nothing. No clothes. He'd arrived without luggage. The only clue that anybody *had* been there *at all* was the empty glass into which his nightcap - a tot of brandy - had been poured.

Under the tumbler was a note.

It was an account detailing how he, Knowles, had come across the unfortunate Daniel, had tried in vain to save him, but confirming that Daniel had died at the scene but with no body as evidence. Knowles had thought of everything. At least Bessie had written proof *from an eye witness* of the tragic event. It was addressed to 'The Coroner, Tavistock'. Next to the written declaration he'd left another saying, to Bessie, 'you might need this'. It referred to the fact that she might need proof of death so a death certificate could be issued. Otherwise, she would have to wait for a statutory seven years before he was officially dead.

He signed it using only his initials followed by an address: 'Deancombe'.

A church service was held to celebrate the life of Daniel William Sercombe two week later, blessing his memory. There was no body and, therefore, no grave or gravestone, so it was agreed there would be a commemorative stone laid for him.

The service was well attended by neighbours and people Daniel knew from the market. They'd travelled from Tavistock. 'Neighbours' were anyone from as far afield as five miles from the farm. That was usual on the moor although, to expect people from five miles as the crow flies to be referred to as 'neighbours' - in the city - would have been impossible. In this part of the moor, as everywhere so remote, you knew everyone for as far as the eye could see, even though you might not engage them in conversation more than once a year.

This was usually at Widecombe Fair or Sharberton Horse Sales or afterwards at The Forest Inn.

But Daniel's passing was more than the end of a life. Much more. Without an heir, it would be the last page in the long history of a family who'd always farmed the moor - a line that had stretched back more than three centuries of Sercombes or, as they were often called, originally, Southcombs.

So it seemed at the time, with William also gone.

Bessie returned to the farm after the service - alone. She dreaded her first night in an empty house. George, Millie and Jenny would be with her of course, but they only added to the sense of loss. It was days before severe hunger forced any of the collies to touch a morsel of food. Pining as they were for their beloved master, they clung to Bessie - following her around the house so closely she was in danger of tripping over them. She only just managed to carry out daily chores; the essential ones, at least.

When Daniel was alive any thought of the dogs setting foot up the stairs was totally out of the question. Now they volunteered, and she encouraged them - keeping her company in what had been the master bedroom, spending each night at the foot of the bed. A few days after the service Bessie's cousin did come over from the north moor to help her cope, and to use the guest room; but she soon had to return, adding more to the feeling of emptiness.

At some stage she knew she'd have to attend to the full demands of running a farm - tending to the sheep in the far grazing as well as the Devon Red milkers closer to home.

As for harvesting, the casual labourers that Daniel traditionally used would always be ready and willing, expecting to be called in as and when the workload demanded. This included Romani families who travelled the moor on a year-round routine, picking up short spells of employment at several farms during the ever-changing seasons. They had perfected the skill of turning up at exactly the right time, exactly when needed.

It was one such 'knock on the door' she'd expected when the dogs began barking furiously on a late summer morning.

But the caller was no gypsy.

'Mrs Sercombe?' asked the caller as she opened the door. The dogs rushed past her skirts to see who it was, sniffing the coat tails of the middle-aged man as he raised his hat in polite greeting.

'Am I addressing Mrs Beatrice Sercombe?'

'Why...yes,' she replied, hesitantly, since she didn't recognise the caller but remained puzzled that *he* seemed to know *her*.

'My name is Barker - Clarence Barker. I represent the estate of the Duchy of Cornwall. It's a matter of business. May I come in?'

With the collie's showing great interest in the

visitor, Barker himself seemed reluctant to invite himself inside, but Bessie agreed, at the same time reaching for one of Daniel's canes. She showed him into the kitchen. In the absence of Daniel she was, for the first time, very aware of her need to be careful.

'I'm sorry to turn up unannounced,' he began, 'but I felt a personal visit would be more appropriate than a simple letter, in the circumstances, in case you had some questions.'

'Circumstances? Questions? Not sure I follow you, Mr...Baker?'

'Barker. Clarence Barker,' he repeated. 'From the Duchy.' Barker handed over his card and the envelope he'd been carrying, adding, 'It's all in there.'

Bessie took the mysterious envelope from Barker, breaking the Duchy seal before taking out the document. She put on her spectacles to examine its contents, reading the first few lines before skipping to the middle part in bold type. It showed dates and reference to 'severance' and 'vacated by' but without really explaining its significance.

'What does it all mean?' she asked, peering over her wire rims to Barker, who already seemed ready for the question before it had left her lips.

'I'm afraid it means you have to leave.'

'*Leave?* Leave where?' She dreaded the answer.

'The farm. Here. You have to leave the farm. By December 21st to be exact. All of it.'

'All of it? What about...?'

'Your stock and belongings?' His readiness with answers told her he'd obviously done this before.

'Well, yes.' It was just then that she realised she was more worried about George, Millie and Jenny than anything else - than any material possessions.

'You must take whatever is yours, and that you wish to keep, by December. Anything else of value can - or should I say, will - be sold at auction. At Rendells. That's why we're giving you notice well in advance. To organise things. Make arrangements.'

As many times as Barker had performed this unfortunate task he still found this part upsetting. He was not a cruel or unfeeling person.

But he had a job to do.

'Why? Why do I have to leave?' she pleaded. 'What have I done wrong?'

'It's not what you've done, Mrs Sercombe, it's what your husband...'

'Well, you got that wrong,' she bit back indignantly, 'he can't have done nothing. He's been dead these past five weeks.'

'Exactly,' said Barker. 'That's the problem. He died - and, please accept my condolences for your recent loss - but he died leaving you with no man to run the farm.'

'Don't need no man,' she retorted. 'I can cope.'

'I'm so sorry,' he leant forward to catch her hand, hopefully to console or reassure her, but she snatched it away. He continued. 'I'm sure you can...cope. But that's not the issue. It's the law. The terms of your tenancy. You have to have a man - a husband, son, or male relative - working the farm with you.

'Living here with you.'

Again, his words only served to bring home how alone she was and how desolate her plight. She buried her face in her apron as the tears flowed. Barker, too, felt the hopelessness of her situation, blowing his nose as emotion got the better of him. It wasn't the first time he'd moved someone to tears.

He hated himself. 'I wish I could...,' he began. But the words failed him.

Bessie sat, straightened herself in her chair, dried her eyes, then requested Barker to sit too.

'How long have I got?'

He was unsure where this was taking him. 'How long before...what, Mrs Sercombe?'

Clarence Barker had left the farm some half an hour later, a little calmer as well as refreshed by a cup of Bessie's dark brown Ceylon tea, enhanced by a liberal helping of brandy. By the end of his visit he'd been more in need of it than Bessie. He was certainly impressed by her sense of enterprise and her questions, both of which proved to him that there was a woman ready to consider all her options before admitting defeat. She was far from a lost cause.

As Barker had said, *she had to find a man.*

The solicitor's chambers were dark and musty, lit by one solitary oil lamp and supported by a thin strip of sunlight from the narrow window. William's eyes had yet to become accustomed to the darkness, and so he was startled when the cloak in the shadowy corner of the room actually moved. A lined, thin-faced figure rose from behind the desk, removing his top hat before reaching across with outstretched hand.

'You must be William Sercombe?'

'I am the same.' The stranger's hand was cold.

'Dare I ask if you carry any proof of that?'

'You may,' William replied, 'and I have.'

He handed over an envelope, sliding it across the leather inlaid desktop. Its contents were his most recent discharge papers from the King's Royal Navy. But William was still mystified by the figure, why he'd tried to trace him, and puzzled by the wording in the classified 'Notices' column of the Bristol Post.

'It said in The Post a meeting would be financially rewarding. For me,' he said, 'and you'd reimburse my travel expenses.'

'Both are correct, young man.' The dark figure chuckled at William's directness. 'I met your father - I'm sorry to say, *just* before he died.

'*He* asked me to find you.'

'My father's...dead?'

The loss of his father was news to William. He was stunned, his blood running cold and draining from his face. 'Do you mind if I sit?' he asked.

The cloaked figure pointed to the seat opposite.

It had been fifteen years since William and Daniel had spoken, or should I say argued, ending in a disagreement that would lead to William leaving the farm to join the navy. It was all coming back to him. It wasn't until later - after he'd had time to cool down and to grow up - that he realised he'd been wrong.

But now it was too late for reconciliation. Daniel was gone. *He was the sole surviving heir.*

Chapter Five

Pride, and the service to the King that he'd signed up to, prevented him returning to make amends with his father. He'd been young, inexperienced, and no more than a boy but he was ambitious and had great ideas for the farm. Daniel, either through lack of desire or uncertainty, had refused to listen. To Daniel, progress was keeping things as they were and how they'd always been. How many times since had William told himself he'd return one day?

Now it was too late.

'And my mother?'

'Gone, I'm afraid. Ten years ago. Scarlet fever.'

'The farm?' William questioned.

'Lost, too, unless...'

'Unless what?'

'Unless you go back - *and soon.*'

'Could I ask to whom I'm addressing?' William was amazed at his own politeness and calmness.

'They used to call me Weaver Knowles.'

'Used to...?

'It's a long story,' said Knowles. 'One that doesn't concern you.' Instead, he placed two tickets before William. 'One is for the stagecoach leaving at noon. For Tavistock.'

'Two tickets? You're coming with me?'

'Only in spirit,' said Knowles. 'I want no payment for the service of acquainting you with your late father's estate, but there is a reason for that. In Tavistock you will contact Willesford's. They're handling his will. All will be made clear then.

'As for the *two* tickets, once you've concluded business in Tavistock I wish you to do me a favour. I have a request, and I must have your word you will carry it out to the letter.'

William was now more mystified than ever. 'That rather depends on what it is,' he answered.

'Very well,' said Knowles. 'But it's simple enough. It involves a hound.'

'A...hound?'

'A hound,' Knowles confirmed. 'But a very special hound that I wish you to feed, look after, and keep with you always at the farm - assuming all goes well at Willesford's and you do take over the tenancy. But you must act quickly on that, or you'll lose it.'

'Yes, of course.' The task seemed simple enough to William. 'Where is this...?'

'The hound will be waiting for you at the Coaching House in Buckfastleigh,' said Knowles. 'The second ticket will take you there. To Buckfastleigh. But there's one more thing I wish you to do, which is *the* most important part of it all.

'Before you take possession of the farm, or even go there, I want you to walk with the hound around the town of Buckfastleigh. Choose a Sunday, either before or straight after the church service when most people are out and about. There I want you to take three circuits of the town, on foot, with the hound beside you on a firm lead. Everyone must *see* what you're doing, but you must speak to no-one about *why* you are doing it, nor discuss this with anyone, before or after.'

'But...?'

'You don't *need* to know why, but I will tell you anyway,' said Knowles. 'The people in the area have been made to fear a large black hound. There are several false stories circulating about the pool at Deancombe being haunted, and of travellers being terrorised by such a hound at the dead of night. It's all untrue, of course.

'The only way to dispel such rumours is by demonstrating to the townsfolk that there *is* a black hound, but that it is harmless. That's where you come in. Simply walk the hound in full view of everyone so that they can see he is as docile as a lamb. You may allow them - any that are brave enough - to approach the hound and even stroke him, but *you* must remain silent. And if they ask, whatever you do say nothing of our meeting, how you came by the hound, and at all costs *never mention me by name.*

'Do we have a deal, Mr Sercombe?'

'Uh...yes. I suppose we do,' said William, but he couldn't disguise the fact he found the whole affair weird. He sealed the arrangement with a final handshake, but not before taking an oath on the Bible that he would keep his word.

William had an hour to spare before the stagecoach was due to leave Bristol, long enough for him to collect enough clothing and essentials from his lodgings. Until this... opportunity... came along he'd taken only temporary diggings with the intention of signing up for the next suitable merchant vessel bound for America. His military rank qualified him for a position as Second Officer, at least, so it was just a matter of time before the right ship came along.

Now this venture had interrupted his plans.

But what did he have to lose? All he had to do was to see what fate awaited him at Willesford's - and follow orders. He was used to that, at least.

There were no coachmen to be seen so he guessed - and he was right - they were inside the lounge bar enjoying a jar or two of ale before embarking on the first stage of the journey. It would take the best part of three days before they arrived at Tavistock. Three very dry days. He checked to make sure he had the tickets safe in his waistcoat pocket before getting straight onto the coach, happy to wait for the noon departure. And the chance to think.

Two coachmen emerged from the Coaching House with just three minutes to spare. After checking his ticket they climbed up to their seats, stirring the team of four into action. They were on their way.

The three day journey involved two nights in

coaching inns as well as frequent stops - 'stages' - to pick up passengers and mail from towns along the way. The first part of the route swept gently down from Bristol into the Somerset levels, then on to the coastal towns of Weston-Super-Mare and Burnham-on-Sea before heading inland to Bridgwater. Next it was Taunton then southwards, missing Exeter to take a less travelled road across country to Crediton and the moors. From Okehampton they dropped down into Tavistock by which time William - as well as the coachmen - were glad to reach the end of their journey, looking forward to a two night break.

That suited William, enabling him to complete business at the solicitors before taking the same coach on the third day, to Buckfastleigh via Plymouth.

The rolling of the coach had been no test for William since he'd suffered much more turbulence, pitch and yaw of naval vessels for the past fifteen years. In fact, initially he'd felt rather at home again with the constant motion helping him to doze. But during his waking hours - especially the long days of empty countryside - his mind had been filled mainly with past memories as a farm boy growing up on Dartmoor. He recalled how those blissful hours and early years with his mother and father *had* been filled with love and happiness after all, and it was the good times that occupied his thoughts the most.

Less happy times, those immediately before his

departure, were now reflected upon with a double sadness - partly filled with regret for having caused so much division in the first place, partly because it was now too late to make amends.

Then there was the loss of his mother. How *had* his father coped after the loss of his wife? Before he left, William had reached an age where his value as a labourer, not short in strength and stamina of a grown man, was something upon which Daniel had begun to rely. Daniel's latter years were lost to William on so many counts, especially since - as he was soon to discover - Daniel had remarried after a period of mourning. Other 'discoveries' might still be out there waiting for him, but only if his appointment at the solicitor's went well.

There he would hear his father's last will and testament.

'Technically you are dead, of course, Mr Sercombe,' the solicitor began. 'The Duchy have petitioned that all rights to the farm, in essence the tenancy agreement, be nullified and returned to them due to you, apparently, being lost at sea for a period exceeding seven years.

'Which we now know to be false,' he added, 'as long as you can prove that you are your father's son.'

'Here are my papers, my discharge papers from the King's Navy together with a record of my severance pay. Note my signature on the receipt.'

'So you can write, Mr Sercombe?' There was air of disbelief in the solicitor's tone, so used to non-professional people having to resort to a mere 'X', rather than a written signature under their name.

'And read,' William confirmed, if only as a warning that he was fully capable of checking the terms of the will.

'Very good,' replied the solicitor clearing his throat, 'then you'll be familiar with this confirmation in writing of a verbal oath you have given to a Mr... errr... Knowles... errr... concerning a dog.'

'Hound,' corrected William. 'I understand he is an Irish Wolfhound I'm to collect in Buckfastleigh.'

'Quite.' The solicitor was unused to be corrected on a matter of fact, merely pointing to a place at the base of the document for William to sign.

'So the farm comes to me now?' William had assumed that his entitlement to the tenancy was what Knowles had meant by 'financially rewarding' but, in the way the solicitor was about to describe his circumstances, it wasn't so straightforward.

'Yes and No. Did you know your father remarried, Mr Sercombe?'

William did. Knowles had told him beforehand making it a double shock. Knowles had informed him his birth mother had succumbed to scarlet fever. But he'd said nothing about a step-mother - a *new* wife.

'So the farm's not mine? But hers... this...'

'Beatrice Sercombe? Not quite. Let me explain.'

The solicitor did explain. He was speaking *to* William but also speaking *for* his deceased father and interpreting Daniel's letter of intent, in his capacity as solicitor and executor of his will.

'So you see,' concluded the solicitor, speaking in terms that William would understand rather than the legal jargon of the will document, 'you have control of the farm - as well as having to meet the conditions of the tenancy agreement, including rent - but your... step-mother retains full rights of occupancy.'

'You mean she can live there?' asked William.

'If she so wishes,' added the solicitor. 'Which I understand she does. And receive a living allowance. Most importantly, it was an express wish of your late father as outlined in his will.'

'But she's not here - now,' quizzed William.

'No. I felt it inappropriate for me to see her before you or, rather, *more* appropriate that I explain things fully *to you, first*. I've known your dear father for many years now and I wanted - for my own personal peace of mind - to be sure that you'd stay faithful to his wishes. Mrs Beatrice is in a very fragile state right now, as you must appreciate, so you must give me your word you will treat her kindly.'

William was struck by the change in the solicitor's tone, his compassion, and demonstrable fondness for his father.

Or at least he *had* been.

William didn't hesitate. 'Yes. Of course I'll look

after... Beatrice.'

William set out for Buckfastleigh the following day ready to meet his obligation to Knowles regarding the hound, feeling positive towards his obligation to his step-mother. It had been his father's last wish so he'd do his best to honour it. It provided him with a connection - one final connection - with his father, to add to the fond memories he still held. But things might not have gone quite as smoothly had it not been for the intervention of Knowles in the first place. Thanks to him, William was fulfilling Daniel's dying wish to save the farm for Bessie, even with his final breath.

The air was crisp as he boarded the morning stagecoach for Buckfastleigh. September sunshine soon took over, bathing the moor in a softness that brought out the best of its colours - the yellow of the gorse contrasting with the heather and the rich greens of the bracken. He remembered how even the air smelled differently once they'd left Crediton a couple of days earlier. He might even have said 'tasted', its balmy scents were so pungent.

Two hours later they were crossing Roborough Downs before their descent into Plymouth, heading to The Barbican.

The city was a hive of industry and brought back memories to William. It almost felt like home, or a second home at least, even though he'd lived there previously for just a few months. But it was the *fond memories* that made him feel so; cherished memories of the first girl he'd ever loved - and still did, if he was honest. She'd been his sanctuary and the refuge to which he'd escaped, or so he'd regarded it during those first days immediately after leaving the farm, some fifteen years earlier.

As the coach pulled in for its stop-over, he took advantage of the break in the journey to call in to one of his favourite haunts - The Dolphin Hotel. In truth, it was little more than an inn offering limited accommodation for sailors and merchants passing through. But the bar was where he'd found solace and companionship - largely from those also on an itinerant path, looking for work and opportunities of less noble a nature. But William had found something else much more appealing - some*one* else.

He'd noticed her as soon as his eyes had grown accustomed to the dimly-lit saloon. She'd served him with his first jar of scrumpy, fascinated as to how a young man so young, well-dressed and well-spoken - and so handsome as she admitted to him later - should be found in a place frequented by those less fortunate. For it was true, his schooling for the years prior to his leaving to work on the farm had been at Tavistock School. His higher education could be credited to the scholarship he'd earned.

It proved to be a poisoned chalice, however, as his

advanced schooling nurtured ideas that created the division between himself and his father. It was the same division that led him to drinking with the strange mixture of rough trade, most of whom were simply biding time until the next sip. (Sorry, *ship!*)

She was the landlord's daughter and, like himself, was barely sixteen years of age, thrust rudely into the world of those much older, and much more worldly. It was hardly surprising they formed an immediate friendship that led, inevitably, to romance. Now, fifteen years later, he reflected on those troubled days, but laced with happy hours where the time together was all too short - walking out with his first love.

He'd always known her as 'B'. He had no idea what it stood for, she wouldn't tell him but it was what everyone called her. As a joke at first, but it stuck, he also referred to himself as 'B' - short for Billy. And so there they were - the two 'B's' - with so many anecdotes, adjectives and adverbs about birds and bees at our disposal to describe how their relationship blossomed.

But just as fierce, strong and passionate as their romance grew, so it was short - *cut* short by accident and circumstance beyond their control.

Isn't that always the case?

Chapter Six

His original intention had been to sign up to the first merchant ship bound for the Americas. Meeting 'B' changed all that. Even if he'd wanted to leave so she, as she said on many an occasion, wouldn't let him. He didn't take much persuading but he needed work, which he found easily on the docks. Up to that point, life on the farm had made him fit and strong and used to long hours. Loading and unloading merchant vessels proved to be easy.

He'd forgotten about a career at sea, but it seemed that life at sea hadn't forgotten about him. Fate took a hand. A day's labour on the docks was thirsty work which, coupled with his thirst to see his beloved 'B', often meant he spent most of his time, between working and sleeping, at The Dolphin. He now felt at home with 'the rough trade' as he called it. Fellow drinkers accepted him so he became complacent about the dangers lurking under the surface of a seaport from those with less than good intentions.

Those dangers included notorious press gangs.

War with France was raging and the Royal Navy was always short of crew for their warships. They had little option but to 'impress' fit and able men to crew their ships. But enthusiasm for earning the King's shilling could only be obtained by force, exerted by gangs looking look for an unfortunate, worse for wear after an evening's drinking. Hence they'd 'press' them into service and be rewarded by the Crown.

Kidnap might be a more appropriate term.

And so it was that fate decided to separate the two 'B's', dictating that William should fall victim to the press gangs. It had been just another evening after work, with William spending his time drinking at The Dolphin so that he could be close to 'his B'. He was waiting for her to complete her evening shift, after which they planned a stroll along The Hoe. But it was not to be. Meanwhile he was relieving himself of his first two jars of cider in the alleyway behind The Dolphin when the press gang struck.

There were five of them, used to over-powering their prey using two advantages - surprise as well as their combined strength. Not that he knew anything about it until he awoke much later with a lump the size of an egg on the back of his head. The hold of the ship was dark until his eyes became used to it. There were others lying next to him, also shackled. Then he felt the unfamiliar rocking of the vessel into which he'd been 'conscripted'. The HMS Undaunted was powering its way out of Plymouth Sound helped by the outgoing tide and a stiff westerly breeze. After the blow on the head he'd been drugged to keep him quiet longer and to make it easier for him to be carried onboard. He'd only regained consciousness after the ship had sailed.

'B' was frantic when she heard from one of the

regulars what had happened, but she knew his plight was useless. It was like a prison sentence from which there was no escape. He'd be held a virtual captive like so many others until resignation and acceptance of their fate took over and, with months and sometimes even years between docking at a home port, they forgotten about home.

William had fallen victim to the same fate.

And, so it was he became lost - lost to the one he loved, missing her so much it almost felt like a bereavement. At first he languished in self-pity, a place where he found many a companion with whom to share his plight. His only salvation was his youth and strength, as well as his determination. He vowed that he would find her again when, as he told himself, 'it was all over'.

But when would that be? With destiny no longer his own, he decided to realise his original ambition, at least, and to learn the ropes. Literally. It paid off. He found he was a natural sailor, able to read the weather - courtesy of growing up on Dartmoor - as well as understanding the sea with her tides and currents. Also, partially due to his intelligence and education gained alongside those who might be considered his betters, he developed natural leadership qualities.

This was soon recognised by his superiors who harnessed his skills and enthusiasm by promoting him to a higher grade. As a result, even if it didn't totally mask his nagging loss and yearning for 'B', at least it gave him some ambition.

But one day he vowed he would escape.

The irony was, some years later when he wasn't on board a fighting ship and no longer a prisoner, he would become jailer himself. He was on shipboard escorting the captured Napoleon to exile on Elba.

From there he was commissioned for more duties in the colonies. Ultimately, it meant that he would almost become used to life without, and beyond, the green fields of England with its unique smells, tastes and sights. Including those of his beloved Dartmoor.

And without his beloved 'B'.

For her part, she learned to forget - she *had to* forget - Billy; her 'B'. But it was equally hard. Her loss, too, was almost tangible, with no respite. No relief or release, despite her vain attempts to trace him. Or ability to send word to him.

So, when her cousin sent word for her to join her for the summer to help out on her farm, she leapt at the chance. Billy had already told her stories of his former life on Dartmoor and on the farm, so she hoped it would make her feel close to him again. He'd described so many people and places to her, as soon as she arrived on the more she felt at home. Although she didn't understand why at the time, it would be a feeling that never left her.

Billy - *William* - had been gone a year.

Chapter Seven

The first summer passed quickly for Bessie, with September and the day of Widecombe Fair soon upon them. It was the highlight of the farming calendar for most. For some, it was the one time of the year they might see a distant neighbour to actually talk to, and the only time they might spend any amount of leisure time, even with those who farmed nearby.

The opportunity to enter a prize bull, calf or White Faced Dartmoor for Best of Breed was secondary. The main purpose was the time for celebration, catching up with the news - a year's worth for some! - dancing and drinking.

And, for a few, meeting a future wife or husband.

Taking place on the second Tuesday in September, the Fair was an all day event culminating in a dance in the village hall next to the church. It was to The Old Inn first that B - Bessie or, to give her full name, Beatrice - arrived with her cousin and husband for a couple of jars, intending to cross the square to the dance, later. The hall was packed but she barely knew anyone apart from one face that looked familiar. Even though they'd never met, she was drawn to him. She forced herself not to stare, but on one occasion he caught her out, looking at him. That was enough.

He was coming over!

Her cousin stepped up to greet him first.

'Bessie,' she said, 'this is Daniel Sercombe. He

owns the farm across the valley from ours. Just outside Pauntry. Daniel; this is my cousin, Bessie.'

Bessie flushed, unable to hide her embarrassment at being caught out. Daniel put her immediately at ease, taking responsibility for their fascination in each other. 'Forgive me for staring,' he said, 'but not only are you the most charming young lady in the room, but I feel I know you. Have we met?'

Bessie flushed even more, if that were possible.

'I don't think that's possible,' she began, 'not unless you frequent Plymouth.'

'Not at all, I regret to say,' said Daniel. 'Never been there. Is that where you come from?'

'I've lived there all my life. This is my first visit to Dartmoor.' She was becoming more at ease.

'Not your last, I hope.'

'No, sir, I'm enjoying it immensely, and even more now that I've...' she broke off immediately, amazed at the admission she was about to make.

Daniel made it easier for her. 'Just as I am so pleased to have met you...Bessie.'

But *why* did Daniel look so familiar to her? And, as for Daniel, how come he'd been so drawn to Bessie - notwithstanding that she was the most attractive - unattached - girl at the dance?

They chatted, oblivious to anyone else in the bar and it was quite obvious they saw *something* in each other. What that *something* was, seemed unclear at first, even though Bessie was the most attractive girl in the bar. It was a feature not lost on local lads who normally knew all the girls in the area, as well as some further afield in Ashburton, Bovey Tracey or Princetown.

They were envious and mystified as to how this old fellow, who must be in his mid-forties, at least, could hold the attention of a maid not yet in her twenties. Even Daniel himself was amazed at his good fortune to meet someone with whom he made an instant connection.

'Where did you say you were staying?' Had he already asked that? Daniel waited for her reply as she took her time, all the while wondering why she felt him so compelling; so familiar to her.

'Ummm... oh... I've been staying at my cousin's for the summer - working, actually.' But her mind seemed to be elsewhere. It wasn't just his face, his mannerisms and expressions, but his voice that she recognised. There was even a touch of sophistication in the way he spoke, despite his distinct moorland dialect.

'Then I might be seeing more of you,' he added with a hopeful note in his voice. She seemed drawn into him even more, replying without thinking what she was saying, words escaping before she knew it.

'Yes. I truly hope so.'

At that point her cousin came over to break into their conversation, but unaware how totally absorbed they were in each other.

'We're off to the dance shortly.'

Bessie held his gaze, fixing her eyes on Daniel as he, too, continued to take in all her features. Breaking the spell she turned to her cousin. 'I'm sorry. I have such a headache. Do you mind if I go home?'

Before her cousin could answer, Daniel took his opportunity. 'Perhaps I can escort you.'

'It's quite a long...'

'I have the pony and trap with me. We don't have to walk.'

How could she refuse - even if she wanted to? Her cousin didn't believe her one bit about her alleged headache but still went along with it, knowing Bessie would be safe in his hands.

The couple made their way through the crowded bar to the back door leading to the where Daniel's rig was waiting for them. It was a typical September evening, if there was such a thing. Away from the gas street lamps of the town, on a night of low dense cloud, it could be so dark that you couldn't see more than a yard in front of you, even at a walk. On the other hand, on a full moon and and with a cloudless sky, it could be so bright that you could, literally, read a newspaper by its light.

Bessie and Daniel were blessed with the latter. It couldn't have been a more perfect setting for their first precious hours together.

They were married the following Spring.

Initially Bessie's father was wary at his beloved daughter becoming betrothed to someone his own age. However, given that Daniel was a man of means and, after several social meetings, had proven himself to be sincere in his intentions, he gave his consent.

Over the course of their courtship, Bessie did learn that Daniel had a son, but that he was lost to him. She dare not delve too deeply into how he was lost, merely accepting that he'd perished while abroad.

Nor did she fully engage with the notion that Daniel's son was one and the same as her 'Billy'. For reasons known only to Billy himself, he'd lied and given her his surname as *Southcomb*. A small change, and a misspelling so common in many family records at the time. But it may have served to preserve his anonymity in case his father sought to find him. However, when press-ganged into service, and still unconscious, his captors had searched his pockets to find the identity of their captive in order to claim reward money. The only evidence was in the form of a prayer book from Tavistock School and the inscription within which bore his name.

So he became William Sercombe again.

But Daniel nor Bessie knew anything of this even though, ironically through a cruel twist of fate, it was William who was the invisible link between them.

Daniel declared later to Bessie that he'd been captivated by her from the start, and that it had been easy for his to fall in love with her. It was a genuine admission, not founded on loneliness at the loss of his first wife who, he also admitted, he would never stop loving, even in death.

Similarly, Bessie's feelings for Daniel went beyond economic or even emotional dependence, anchored as they had always been in a discovery of the same attractions she had found in her Billy, before he was so cruelly taken from her. She'd searched for him through ports' and ships' records, only to be informed via the Royal Navy that most of those conscripted, at the time she specified, had joined the sixteen gun HMS Seagull. It had been captured by the sloop Lougen off Christiansand, but there was no news of the fate of the crew. They were presumed lost, too.

So she'd assumed the worst.

Little did she know that Daniel had also made similar enquiries at the time about his son, only to be given the same response. They were in mourning for the same William, simultaneously, without knowing.

But for entirely different reasons.

In many cases during extended conflicts between nations, naval ships were captured by one country and then recaptured - sometimes by an entirely different country - to maintain the strength of a nation's fleet. Over its lifetime, the same ship could often end up flying under a succession of different flags. But crew members had no value other than to be traded or used as 'swaps' between warring countries. That was the fate that had befallen William whilst he remained signed up to the navy. He'd been captured and traded.

Some ten years after his initial capture (by the press-gang), then his subsequent capture (by the French allies), followed by his recapture by - or return to - the Royal Navy, his visit to Plymouth and The Dolphin where it all began, had left him in sombre mood. In particular, memories of his beloved 'B' were flooding back.

But Weaver Knowles had given him a commission.

His next task in hand, that of collecting the hound at the coach house in Buckfastleigh and parading him around the town, had given him fresh focus. It had been a strange request and seemed even more strange the closer he came to his destination. But he'd given his word and actually signed an oath, promising to fulfil the obligation.

As he approached the drop-off point in the town he could see the hound waiting, held on a short leash by a handler. Was it his imagination or was the hound already wagging its tail in warm greeting? Indeed it was. The large black Irish Wolfhound was responding affectionately to William's voice. He gave into a natural instinct to scratch the dog's ears.

'Hello, boy,' he said, taking over the leash from the handler whilst continuing to fuss over the animal.

He turned to the handler. 'What's his name?'

Knowles hadn't mentioned a name and there was no name tag on his collar. 'No idea,' came the reply.

'Right,' said William as the handler bade him farewell. He addressed the hound, 'then I will have to name you myself. I think I will call you... Colin. Yes, that sounds right.

'Is that OK with you, Colin?'

More wagging of his tail seemed to suggest he'd chosen well and, with that, they began their first circuit of the town. He had three tours to complete after which they could both head home or, at least to the cottage that Willesford's had rented on his behalf. It would be just until he laid official claim to the farm by moving in. Grey Cottage would be a base from which to start and allow him time to make the acquaintance of his step-mother.

In turn it would give *her* time to get used to the idea that her late husband's son was returning from the dead (or so she imagined). It would be hard for her to see a stranger take up residence of what she had considered would still be her home - and hers alone.

But first he must parade the hound - Colin - as instructed by Knowles, around the Buckfastleigh. It began well, with most men tipping their hats respectfully and women offering a discreet bow as he passed them in the street. In less than half an hour he had covered most of the town, including side streets and alleyways.

By the time he'd begun a second circuit there were more people. He assumed it was because word had spread and they were curious to see this unusual stranger. More especially it was to see if it really was the large black hound that, some said, was the very spectre, or ghost, of Weaver Knowles. Not that William would have a clue on that score because he was forbidden to engage townsfolk in conversation.

By the third turn of the town virtually every street was lined with locals. They stood at the front step of their cottages to view this bizarre spectacle. Some ducked back inside while he passed whilst others crossed themselves as a precaution against danger, but they stood their ground. It wasn't until he passed the entrance to the church that a more prominent resident of Buckfastleigh presented himself, waiting for William to appear.

If accounts are to be believed, this prominent person was the one who started the whole thing.

Chapter Eight

It was the local parson. He emerged from the entrance to the churchyard ready with incense and holy water to bless both himself and Colin, in a fashion that resembled an exorcism, seemingly addressing and denouncing evil spirits.

Unknown to William, it *was* the same parson who'd placed a curse on the alleged ghost of Weaver Knowles some years earlier. William thanked him as he passed, whilst Colin gave a brief 'yip' rather than a bark, wagging his tail in acknowledgement - *and recognition* - of the clergyman.

The parson's blood ran cold as he recognised Colin, and he retreated quickly indoors. The rest of the final circuit was without incident.

It was late afternoon when William and Colin were able to take their leave of the town. The stagecoach upon which they'd arrived was long gone, travelling northwards to Exeter and beyond. It fell upon him, therefore, to seek out a local, private carrier with the means and the will to take them to Pauntry at short notice.

'It'll cost you double,' said the driver as William and Colin mounted the carriage. It was small and drawn by a single pony, sufficient for a short journey.

'How come?' William questioned.

'I gotta come back - so it's two trips for me.'

The logic of the argument was lost on William.

'In advance,' added the driver.

Colin growled his disapproval; William paid up.

'And make sure that devil hound is secure,' said the driver, well-briefed by his fellow townsfolk.

After passing through the neighbouring town of Ashburton it was a steady climb up onto the moor, with further gradients - both ascents and descents - to challenge the pony. But she was a young mare and used to the terrain. Like most local horses she'd developed a natural fitness to match the country, as well as the ability to pace herself. They rested for a short time at the new bridge at Hannaford. From that point, the driver asked both William and Colin to walk behind the rig for the steep pull up to The Tavistock Inn at Poundsgate, then once again for the last stretch uphill to Leusdon Common where the ground levelled out.

Once safely at Pauntry they sought out Mrs Westabrook who was to furnish William a key. Grey Cottage was a small thatched two-up, two-down next to the mill house, and the temporary accommodation arranged by Knowles, through Willesfords. He was heartened to discover that Mrs Westabrook had a pot of stew prepared for his supper. She'd covered it with a tea-towel where it sat on the kitchen table together with a loaf, butter, bacon, eggs, black pudding and mushrooms for his breakfast.

Most of all he needed his bed and fell asleep in an armchair in front of the fire, his meal half finished and the hound at his feet, also sound asleep.

Colin remained indoors overnight but that was to be a one-off occurence. Knowles had given him strict instructions not to keep the hound shut inside the house - *any house or barn* - overnight. Colin was to be provided free access in and out of the farmhouse, allowed to roam at his own pleasure even for days on end if he, the hound, so wished.

The only reason Knowles gave was that the hound was a hunter by nature and used to fending for himself. William didn't question the request at the time but, the more he heard tales of a black hound and it's alleged haunting of Deancombe, the more he wondered about the true identity of his charge.

William rose at six o'clock the following morning but only to let Colin out to 'do his business'. The amount of travelling over the recent few days had caught up with him so, after placing a few more logs on the dying embers of the fire, he returned to the armchair and slept until noon.

A late breakfast followed, courtesy of the rations left by Mrs Westabrook, but he decided the remains of the stew would suffice for Colin's next meal, as and when he returned to the cottage. That turned out to be shortly after one o'clock in the afternoon, at which point William himself went for a walk. The air was distinctly chilly and the nights had started to draw in. Summer was coming to an end. After a bright start to the day low cloud descended, blocking the sun but without obscuring his vision at ground level. It was a reminder autumn was just around the corner.

The next day, Tuesday, was the actual Widecombe Fair but Monday was preparation day. Those who weren't making produce to sell on the day, or rehearsing their routines for entering cattle, sheep or other farm animals for the 'Best of Breed', were finishing off essential tasks around their farms. They had to condense two days into one so they could enjoy a so-called day off. Committee members and officials were also busy erecting tents and stands and marking out show rings at the show ground itself.

Everyone seemed to be doing something for or connected to the show. After all it was the highlight of the local calendar and seemed to involve everybody.

Even children had the day off school.

William still had his own boyhood recollection of past days at the Fair. He, too, was looking forward to the day and, for all sorts of reasons, had decided it would be inappropriate to make himself known to the widow at his father's farm until Wednesday, at the earliest. For now, at least, he would enjoy a relaxing walk, taking in the places, if not the people, he remembered from his early days. He decided on a circular walk, clockwise, striking an easy pace uphill towards Sweeton Farm.

Crossing 'the splash', or 'Forder Bridge' as it was referred to by the locals, since you could either cross by *ford, or bridge*, he climbed the stile immediately after to take the path by the River Webburn It ran behind Grey Cottage until reaching the small hamlet of Jordon. There he rejoined a road taking him to the main lane at which point he turned right, back to Pauntry. Luckily, the Post Office Store was open where he was able to buy enough fresh provisions for an evening meal and breakfast, which he preferred, rather than take a trip to The Tavistock Inn for fear it would lead to a late night.

Dawn broke on the Tuesday with a clear sky and bright morning sun promising a dry day. He told himself he would take Colin with him although, judging by the independent streak demonstrated by the hound so far, it was more of a case of whether Colin would *allow* himself to be taken. Either way, they rose early to energise themselves with a decent breakfast before setting out on the two mile hike to the show ground. They arrived soon after eight thirty to find the fair already buzzing with activity. Most of those participating were already there, seeking out friends and neighbours who, in some cases, they only saw socially but once a year.

Uncle Tom Cobley was on his old grey mare, represented this year by one of the Coker family. The village centre and the lanes into Widecombe were lined with carriages, all from outside of the area. Locals elected to be dropped off from whatever means of transport they could organise, to be picked up later at the end of the day. Or they walked or rode.

Folk were arriving from as afar afield as Newton Abbot, Buckfastleigh and Ashburton, Chudleigh and north of the moor from Princeton, Tavistock, Moretonhampstead and Chagford. Even *groups* from towns, villages and organisations had turned up, transported in privately hired omnibuses. They had to be pulled by four horses rather than the usual two, owing to the steep gradient of Widecombe Hill.

Not that it mattered if most of the people came from in country, he knew none of the locals in any case; not even his closest neighbours in the village.

But *they* seemed to know *him*, no doubt because they knew he was coming and he was expected to be there. News travels fast in small communities assisted by a variety of means - notably estate agents, land conveyancers, machinery suppliers and, of course, solicitors. It was a built-in security process evolved by and serving all who lived locally, a safety mechanism in case any unwelcome outside influences appeared on the horizon.

Some had even heard of the black hound itself and William's recent short visit to - *and through* - Buckfastleigh. He could thank the carriage driver for that. His tongue had been loosened, ironically, by the fare with which William had graced him and which, on the way home, he spent liberally at The Tavistock Inn and, later, at The Bay Horse in Ashburton.

William was now recognised as the stranger with the black Irish Wolfhound. Colin had even earned a reputation and notoriety of his own, thanks to the rumours and accounts filtering up from Buckfastleigh. William repaid them with a stint of people-watching.

This diversion of his included matching family members with each other; brothers, sisters, cousins, aunts and uncles. It turned out to be not so difficult as he first imagined, given that the extended family was an essential part in making any rural community work. He also played his own game - although he was the only player - where he tried to guess *who* might be married to *whom* or - and this was more difficult - which couples might be just '*seeing each other*'.

He also found himself taking this one step further, speculating on which players were engaged in liaisons that were less noble (some would say), and relationships not connected by family, marriage, or betrothal. This then led to the inevitable: namely spotting those ladies of a certain marriageable age who were unattached. And (ideally) pretty.

But he wasn't prepared for what was to follow, a chance meeting and discovery that not only brightened his day, but changed his life.

Forever.

'Billy? Is it really you?' called the voice.

Without even looking up to see who it was, he recognised her purely on the strength of those first few words, but he didn't actually believe his ears until he turned to face her.

Then he couldn't believe his eyes.

"B'? Is it really *you*? What are you *doing* here? And so far from home?'

When someone is lost to you but still commands your thoughts frequently and over such a long time - becoming a deep memory - seeing them when you least expect it simply doesn't register. Not at first, especially if they appear out of context.

But it *was* her, as beautiful as he could ever remember, standing before him.

'I thought you were dead,' she said, with almost a hint of anger and sense of betrayal in her tone.

But not in her face.

'I was,' he replied, 'at least, for a while. Captured, first by the English press-gang then by the French, in battle, after which I was returned to the English who sent me abroad. Either way I couldn't escape.'

'I searched for you.'

'I'm sorry. I wasn't allowed to contact anyone back home.'

'I heard you'd been taken, kidnapped, by a press-gang. One of the regulars at The Dolphin told me. He saw it happen but they warned him to keep quiet, or else...' Bessie's tone softened as she recalled her anguish when she'd learnt what had happened to him that night, but only after his ship had sailed.

'I've missed you so much.'

'Whose this handsome young chap then?' Bessie's cousin had been standing nearby and broke into the conversation, clearly impressed by William's bearing and appearance.. 'Not see 'e before, me 'andsome.' She'd just returned from the refreshment bar with her husband, both were now the worse for wear.

'I'm sorry,' said Bessie. 'This is my cousin, Mary, and her husband, Jack.'

'Pleased to meet you,' William said to them, but that was all. It was Bessie who had his total attention. But how she came to be so far from home mystified him. 'Are you visiting... your cousin?'

'Not exactly,' she said, sounding vague, then realising how it might seem strange to him. 'I live *here*, now. On a farm just over Corndon. I own it - at least I used to - until...'

'Then you must be Beatrice. Beatrice Sercombe?' It was a coincidence that stretched his belief in what was happening even further, until she answered.

'Yes, but how did you guess?'

'I'm a Sercombe, too. My father was Daniel Sercombe.'

'My late husband,' she gasped. She thought for a while. 'So you're my...'

'Step-son,' he uttered, barely audible, shocked at first before lapsing into laughter at the absurdity of it all. 'Pleased to meet you at last... mother!'

If the circumstances weren't so strange you could say they *were* laughable - which they were. It was a joke shared by all. But once normality had returned, Mary and Jack excused themselves, aware the two had much catching up to do.

'I called in at The Dolphin,' he said once they were alone. 'You weren't there. I didn't really expect you to be, but I thought I might see your father.'

'He's been passed away some five years,' she replied. 'Seems like everyone around me has died, or been lost.' She was referring to Daniel, and then to himself, of course.

'It was a shock to me, too,' he said. 'First my mother, then dad. I know dad and I were hardly what you'd call close towards the end, but he was a good man, and a good father.'

'And a good husband,' she whispered. 'I will always miss him.'

'Then we shall miss him together,' he added.

She caught his hand. 'What shall we do now?' It was rather an ambiguous question she'd asked.

'I hadn't really thought about it.' He corrected himself immediately. 'That's not true. I had it all worked out, expecting a much older woman, of course, but not expecting my father's widow to be my... *to be you*. But seeing it *is* you, and that we used to...' He stopped for fear of saying something stupid.

He'd run out of ideas.

'Where are you staying?' Bessie was trying to change the subject, or at least bring clarity to what exactly they *were* talking about.

It only forced them to think of the inevitable: *Where would* she *stay, if* he *were to live at the farm?*

'I can have Grey Cottage for as long as I like, I suppose,' he said. 'The solicitor put me up there intending to help me settle into the area before taking over at the farm, but I imagine I could rent it.'

The 'taking over the farm' statement seemed a little brutal, too harsh a reality, one he'd been keen to avoid and protect his new step-mother's pride and sensitivities. But Bessie didn't see it like that.

'Or you could buy it,' said Bessie. 'I heard someone say it was part of the estate of some weaver fellow from Dean Prior way. Willesford's is executor. Why don't you ask them - that's if you intend staying?'

Why would she even *think* he wasn't staying?

The uncertainty in her voice betrayed the fact that she *wanted* him to stay; not lose him a second time.

'Yes, of course. Good idea,' he agreed. She then posed the *real* question, one for which she dreaded the answer.

'Can we sit down for a moment, Billy? Or should I call you 'William'?' she began.

'William is fine, Bessie,' he said as he joined her on a bench overlooking what had been the collecting ring for the novice jumping. It gave them the privacy they needed but, most of all, a quietness away from the crowds. Time to think.

She continued.

'You know I can't stay at the farm on my own, don't you?'

'Do you mean that tenancy thing, where a woman can't take responsibility for a farm without a man?'

'Yes,' she replied. 'I've already had one visit from the Duchy. They want to find a new tenant and throw me out.'

'I know.' Now he took *her* hands in *his* to reassure her; this time she flushed at the sign of familiarity. He explained how he'd been set on this course after his meeting with the mysterious figure in Bristol.

'Have you heard of a fellow called Knowles?' Colin's ears twitched at the sound of his name, then settled again, but listening more intently.

'Can't say that I have,' she replied.

If hounds could express disappointment, Colin would have. The nearest he came to it was a deep sigh, resting his chin upon his outstretched paws.

William continued.

'Well, he knew my father, apparently. It was Knowles who told me of Daniel's dying wish.' She grasped *his* hands now, and tighter. 'He wanted you to be looked after with him gone and, at all costs, you weren't to lose the farm.

'He put out a search for me in the Bristol Post. Lord knows how he even knew I existed, let alone that I was in the area. *He* told me, explaining that, if I could prove I was Daniel's lost son, there was a good chance I could lay legal claim to take over the tenancy. But with you still able to stay.

'If you want to, that is...' He looked deeply into Bessie's eyes for the answer *he* needed to hear, and the one *she* wanted to give him.

'I want nothing else.' Her eyes moistened as she saw her torment coming to an end. 'But how will this work? It wouldn't look right, two of us living together, even if we agreed not to...'

'You're right, for now, at least,' he said.

But what *did* he mean by 'How *would* it work'? And why did he say 'for now'? She needed something more permanent. Lasting.

Chapter Nine

They continued walking and talking. It made them feel less conspicuous in a way, moving anonymously through the crowd and still able to talk freely, breaking off now and again to take in the show. But they both knew there were still questions left unanswered. William decided to take the lead in resolving them. If she agreed, they could move on.

Together.

'As I see it,' he said, 'we have to make sure the farm doesn't revert back into the hands of the Duchy. Willesford's should be able to secure it for us, now they can prove that I, as legal heir, am alive.'

'But, where does that leave me?'

'I'll instruct Willesford's to draw up a declaration for me to sign, declaring that you have full rights of occupancy and enjoyment of residence while I still live. That will be your guarantee that there will always be a home for you at the farm.'

'In your lifetime,' she added.

He could see her point, and why she hesitated.

'It's the best I can do,' He wished he could think of something better. 'But there's no way round it *unless I have an heir*.'

That sparked something else on her mind.

'Will you stay with me, William?'

'Do you think that's a good idea?' he asked, even though he knew it was what they both wanted. But he realised it would be so frowned upon by the villagers that they would risk being shunned.

'I'll stay in Grey Cottage,' he said. 'Officially, anyway. Permanently.'

She knew he was right.

A week later he was in Willesford's to sign papers and transfer £75 for the purchase of Grey Cottage.

'You know the owner, Mr Knowles, of course - don't you, Mr Sercombe?' The solicitor couldn't help noticing the recognition of Knowles' name by the black hound, but he said nothing.

'Knowles?... yyy-es, of course,' stuttered William. Naturally he knew Knowles, but he was still surprised to learn that he'd been the owner of Grey Cottage. But it made sense. Willesford's were the executors of Knowles' estate as well as Daniel's.

What made even more sense was for William to buy, rather than rent, the cottage. As the owner rather than tenant of the cottage, he inherited cottager's and commoner's rights. They not only gave him a firmer stake in the community, but he had use of the moor for grazing. More importantly it preserved Bessie's reputation if he were seen to have a separate residence, despite spending so much time at the farm. Neither of them could resist the temptation to renew their relationship as it had been before they became lost to each other, but they still had to be careful not to be seen to be too familiar. But they took risks.

'I wish I didn't have to go back to the cottage each night,' he sighed as they lay back together in the hay loft. There was a sheet missing on the barn roof above them, affording them a glimpse of clouds scudding across the sky after a sudden shower. They'd run for cover but not without getting soaked. Not for the first time did the inevitable happen after they'd quickly had to dispense with their wet clothes.

They had a lot of lost time to make up for...

'You'd better get out there in any case,' she said. 'The dairyman will be arriving to collect today's milk any time now. And I still have the chickens to feed. He mustn't catch us like this.'

She draped a blanket round her before heading back to the farmhouse. He found a dry smock hanging up to replace his drenched shirt, but had to settle for wet trousers. He crossed the yard to the milk shed where two churns were already loaded on a handcart. It was a slight sloping driveway down to the front gate where he left the milk each day, so he didn't need to lift them onto the pony and trap.

He'd soon settled into the daily routines, finding it strange at first to be taking orders from Bessie - which he did willingly until he'd learnt the ropes. But the hardest thing to get used to, for both of them, were the long nights apart. He already knew that 'everybody knew everybody else's business' in a rural community such as this. And, what the locals didn't know they made up, with stories that stretched the imagination as well as the truth.

For those reasons he accepted that it would be foolish to take risks by sleeping over. But, as winter closed in and the sun rose later in the day, it became easier for him to sneak under cover of darkness earlier than his usual six o'clock, to seek the comfort of her warm bed.

He would stay for his evening meals after most of the daily chores were finished, easily persuaded to stay for 'just a little bit longer' afterwards. They would sit together watching the flames lick round the dry logs in the inglenook. He would be enjoying a jar or two of their home-made cider; she busying herself with her knitting needles, just as she had done so many times with his father. It was hard to believe those days were just a few months ago when Daniel was still alive, and William was still lost to her.

She still wore black on occasions she went to the village, or Newton Abbot market, or to Leusdon Church each Sunday. It seemed right for her to do so. Whatever she and William had embarked upon - had re-embarked upon - her respect for Daniel was still deep. She also felt that she owed it to his memory to demonstrate that respect openly to others.

'I know how you still hold memories of my father,' he said to her as they walked home from church one Sunday. She'd gone over to the memorial stone she'd laid for Daniel, blessing it just after the service. There was no body - it had never been recovered - nor any ashes. But she marked his passing with a stone.

'I understand now that when I first met your father I saw you in him. It was you I was looking for all those years. You *lived* in Daniel.' She paused to wipe a tear away with her handkerchief.

'When will we be able to...?'

'Tell others about us?' she asked, anticipating what he was about to say. But she pondered for a while, giving him some hope, answering only as they climbed upon the pony and trap that stood waiting across from the church gates, making sure they couldn't be overheard.

'Soon. But not yet. Not quite yet. I'm sure people already suspect that we... you know... but it has to feel right. I'll know when I'm ready.

'I shall wait for a sign.'

It was the New Year when the sign came, a sign that she'd half expected, and half hoped for. She'd just returned from a rare visit to her aunt in Plymouth. William felt it unusual since she hardly had any contact with her father's sister, as far as he *knew*.

It turned out to be a visit with a special purpose.

'I'm going to have a baby,' she announced one evening after supper. William was taking a draught of cider and nearly choked on the news. His response needed no thinking about... at first.

'That's wonderful!' he gasped, holding her so tight

she could hardly catch her breath.

'Careful,' she warned. 'You'll squash him...'

'Him?'

'Or her.' she replied. 'Either way, I wanted to be sure. That's why I didn't tell you. Not at first.'

'And that's why you went to your aunt's. To see a doctor, as well?'

'I didn't want our own doctor in Ashburton. The news would spread before had a chance to get...'

'Get married? he whispered, searching her face and hoping it would be the reaction he wanted.

'I was going to say "get back home", but yes. It must be the sign I needed.' With that she flung her arms around him, not needing to say any more. It was all the sign *he* needed, in any case.

And the 'beat, beat, beat' of the black hound's tail told them that they weren't the only ones delighted at the news.

Chapter Ten

They were married within the month.

It was no surprise to her cousin, Mary. Her mother, Bessie's aunt in Plymouth, had already sent word about Bessie's 'condition'. The wedding also took place in Plymouth, a civil ceremony performed by a local JP. To have followed the lengthy process of having the bans read locally it would have meant that, by the time their wedding day arrived, Bessie would have been showing even more. That really would set the tongues wagging. So far, she'd concealed it well.

None of their neighbours on Dartmoor were invited or even told in advance. There seemed no point, or need, since her cousin was the only person to whom she felt close enough to invite. Which she did, as one of the witnesses. It took place with very little arrangement needed, after which it was life back to normal with a farm to run.

But only for William.

They had to come up with a plan to 'postpone' the recorded date of the new baby, if not on paper, then in the eyes of the locals in and around Widecombe. With an aunt who was so accommodating and far enough away had its advantages. Near to Bessie's 'time' she took herself off immediately to Plymouth for the birth, but the idea was for her to stay several weeks *after* giving birth. The last thing they needed was for rumours about them 'having' to get married.

Bessie had to appear to have gone the full nine month term *after* their wedding day.

But they still had to consider how it looked to the wider world. Would they still be seen to have married too soon after the death of Daniel?

Some would say yes, on moral grounds, but they built a story around having to become man and wife without further delay, in order to retain the tenancy to the farm. At least for Bessie's sake. As is turned out, her security really was preserved for the future if William were to pre-decease her. She gave birth to a baby boy, Francis.

They called him Frankie.

He grew up to be a fine lad, following his father's footsteps in many ways, strong boned and with a keen brain, nurtured and developed with a good education thanks to a scholarship to Tavistock School. Just like William. Unlike William, Frankie's true heart stayed on the farm, where he relished summer holidays working side by side with his father. As for Bessie, having the two of them with her, William and Frankie, was all she would ever want.

Colin had also found peace, happiness and a home, on Corndon. He was tolerated by the three border collies, even though he didn't actually 'work' as far as they were concerned. William kept his commitment to Knowles to look after him. But the strange thing was, although George, Millie and Jenny grew visibly older - suffering from arthritis to a point where herding sheep was no longer possible - Colin never seemed to age. His coat kept its sheen, his teeth were healthy and white, his eyes clear, and the hair on his muzzle showed no hint of grey.

He also kept to his routine of going off for days on end, sometimes weeks, on tramps to who-knows-where before returning to the farm, as if it were the most natural thing to do. Of course, for a hound it was. William became used to it, as did Bessie, to the point where she actually missed him when he was gone. But his excursions were not without incident.

How many times (it was so many that William lost count) would there be reports that 'a beast had been seen prowling the moor late at night?' And how often had he sensed the sideways glances directed his way if he happened to be present when such stories were being told, becoming more and more fanciful?

Some stories that circulated in local pubs and on market days in, say, Newton Abbot and Tavistock spoke of a black panther, or a large black cat of some kind, allegedly escaped from a travelling circus. Some even claimed they'd witnessed a spectre changing shape from a human to an animal, ready to prey on young children or on weary or lost travellers.

Others suspected the beast - whatever form it took - to be responsible for the slaughter of sheep or newborn calves. This part *did* worry William in case

Colin was accused of such menace. If that were the case, they were just as likely to shoot him on sight, even without clear evidence.

All William could do was to be vigilant, to keep Colin close to the farm whenever such stories were going round. He also made sure Colin was with him as much as he could during lambing season. Old George had passed away, as had Millie, whilst Jenny was also looking frail and would soon be unable to work. She stayed behind at the farm most days if William had to go out to mend fences or manage hedgerows, if only to keep Bessie company. He was training a new border collie called Young George and made a point to have Colin with them. That way he could learn the dog-sheep relationship. It gave him a chance to watch Colin's behaviour around the sheep, looking for any signs of aggression towards them especially when they had new-born lambs.

So far he'd seen nothing out of the ordinary, which at least gave him peace of mind, and justification for defending Colin if any stock had been taken, with owners looking for a culprit. Any culprit. He was certain Colin would be blameless.

But that suddenly changed.

It happened in the middle of lambing but, on this occasion, whilst checking his neighbour's flock. If one farmer had been out all night, as was often the case, it was common for duties to be shared, and for neighbours to help each other out. It was on one such early morning after a storm that something happened that changed the lives for all at the farm.

William knew it wasn't uncommon for a ewe to give birth in the middle of the night. Frankie was with him, riding his grey gelding, Handsome Boy. William drove the pony and trap. As they entered the pound they took to scouting the walled boundary and the patches of gorse on the perimeter. It would be unusual for a ewe to lamb in *open* ground, preferring to seek protection from predators and cover from any weather blowing in, such as last night's storm.

On this occasion Colin had run on in front, reaching the neighbour's field well ahead of them. William was puzzled at the time that Colin, for some reason, or was it coincidence, instinctively knew where they were going and, apparently, why.

He sat waiting for them when they arrived, but as William approached Colin his mouth dropped.

He saw blood.

Blood was smeared all over Colin's chops and had stained his teeth and paws red. It was clear to see as he lay waiting - panting from excitement or some violent exercise, and for reasons at which William could only guess, as tragic as his suspicions were.

'Curse you, hound,' he seethed. Colin whimpered as if apologetically, but remained still even as William turned back towards the trap for his shotgun.

The next words chilled him to the bone.

'I had to kill it.'

They were not his nor were they from Frankie, who'd trotted over on Handsome Boy to where the carcass of a lamb lay, bloodied and slain. William had picked up his gun, checked the two cartridges in the chambers, and now looked up to see who'd spoken.

Or what.

The words had come from a mouth that was smeared with blood, now a human mouth as were the rest of the form stood before him; hands, not paws, reaching out as if to plead for mercy.

'Knowles?' whispered William, not believing his eyes and the figure *of the man* stood before him.

'But it wasn't me. I didn't do it,' Knowles cried. His shaggy coat had been replaced with a long black cape and his skin was that of a human.

'Stay back,' shouted William, fearful that whatever stood before him, man or beast, might attack him, too. William's gun was trained on... what?

Just then, just in time as William was aiming the barrel at the unfortunate figure and ready to pull the trigger, Frankie called out. He was over where a ewe stood by her recently killed new-born lamb, the remaining, surviving twin. Its sibling was little more than a carcass, but barely feasted upon.

'Stop, father.' He'd seen the transition of Colin as he changed from hound into human; into Knowles.

'He's telling the truth,' Frankie cried.

William lowered the barrel, first looking to his son

for answers to such a claim, then back to Knowles for *his* explanation of events. If Colin - or Knowles - hadn't killed the lamb, then who had?

'There's a fox,' said Frankie as he rode slowly towards them, 'a vixen. She must have cubs to feed. She's dead but still warm. Colin must have come across her attacking the lamb and killed her.

'*He killed the fox, not the lamb.*'

'I had to do it,' said Knowles, with a mix of regret tinged with gratitude that the real culprit, and not him, had been discovered. He looked wretched, older, not the confident man that William had first met in Bristol. And he looked tired. It was as if he'd at last arrived at the end of a long journey - not so much a physical one, but one where he'd been hiding from his true identity - neither one thing nor the other.

Neither man, nor beast.

'I... I don't understand,' muttered William.

'I don't expect you to understand,' sobbed Knowles. 'To be cursed on my death, to live the life of a reviled creature as punishment for my past wrongs committed when alive. Wandering alone for so long. Then to find happiness again with you, Bessie, and master Frankie.

'To finally have a home again.'

'But now this. What am I to do now my secret's out? You might as well shoot me after all, guilty or not. Put me out of my misery.'

'I'm not going to do that,' William reassured him.

'*We*'re not, are we, Frankie?'

'No sir,' replied Frankie with a level-headedness and courage well beyond his years. He turned to Knowles. 'It was you who tried to save my grandfather, was it not? How can *we* ever repay *you*?'

'Just keep my secret. Please. That's all I ask,' said Knowles. He was calmer, recovered from the shock of the transformation over which he had no control.

'Of course,' said William. 'And you can still stay with us, but it will be your choice.'

'My choice? What do you mean?' asked Knowles. 'What *are* my choices?'

'You can be man or hound. You shall decide how to live out the remainder of your life.'

'With us,' added Frankie.

EPILOGUE

So it was that Weaver Knowles served his penance and, after suffering such ignominy during his time living 'in country' and away from the moor, at last he found freedom and safety as well as certainty in later life on a moorland farm.

At least, certainty of identity.

He retained the name Knowles, but dropped the qualifying term 'Weaver', for fear that those who remembered such a person in his former life accused him of deeds and crimes associated with 'the old Knowles'.

Most of all, he was afraid that the curse laid upon him by the parson would return *to haunt him*.

So how did they explain to the locals who their new guest was, and how he came to be there? Bessie, William, and Frankie decided to explain to anyone who asked about Knowles that he was Daniel's long lost cousin. He'd simply had turned up unannounced and they found themselves duty-bound to take him in, given that they were his only family.

Who could dispute it?

At last he'd escaped his past - both as man and beast - and now lived contentedly as the former. As a black hound he'd been immortal; ageless. Living a life again as a human, the years gradually took their toll. Tales of 'the beast of Dartmoor' still grumbled on in the background, with sightings - alleged sightings, that is - continuing to be the talk at the local inns and fairs, off and on.

Nor did they stop at Dartmoor, but cropped up on Exmoor and, occasionally, on Bodmin Moor.

Whether they were our black hound, a puma escaped from a travelling circus, or what? Who knows? Once myth and legend are born and embedded into folklore, it is hard to kill them off. They even become more vivid, illustrated, and believable the more times they are told.

At least Weaver Knowles had a chance to atone for his misgivings, albeit in death - his first death. But even he finally succumbed to the merciless passage of time on this earth.

He became more and more frail.

Knowles passed away peacefully one summer afternoon. Young George was at his feet. He was dozing in the carver set out for him to catch the sun's rays in the front garden, gamely holding onto his favourite tankard. The remains of his cider were gradually warming in the heat of the day.

His eyes were closed. William sat opposite, also suitably furnished with a jar of scrumpy. Bessie's knitting needles clicked away on her latest pattern - a cardigan for Knowles.

Suddenly a squall rustled through the leaves of the

willow tree, before going on to bang the barn door shut; then open it; then bang it shut again.

Knowles stirred in irritation at the disturbance and fought to open his eyes. He sighed deeply.

'What is it, Knowles?' asked William.

Knowles ran his tongue over his dry lips.

'Tell your father... *tell Daniel...* I'm coming.'

He then beckoned William to come closer as if uttering just a few words was an effort.

There was more. He hadn't quite finished.

William leant forward. 'What is it, my friend?'

'I was never keen on the name Colin.'

Knowles had spoken his final words. He slipped away peacefully, a smile remaining on his lips and in his eyes, though they were now closed.

Now he'd finished.

THE END...for now